The Gallows Garden

KENDELL FOSTER CROSSEN
Writing as
M.E. CHABER

With an Afterword by
KENDRA CROSSEN BURROUGHS

STEEGER BOOKS / **2020**

PUBLISHED BY STEEGER BOOKS
Visit steegerbooks.com for more books like this.

PUBLISHING HISTORY

Hardcover
New York: Rinehart & Company, January 1958.
Toronto: Clarke, Irwin & Company, 1958.
London: T. V. Boardman (American Bloodhound Mystery #225), August 1958. Dust jacket by Denis McLoughlin.

Paperback
New York: Pocket Books #1240, as *The Lady Came to Kill*, May 1959. Cover by Len Goldberg.
New York: Paperback Library (63-549), A Milo March Mystery, #18, March 1971. Cover by Robert McGinnis.

ISBN: 978-1-61827-515-8

To Lisa Palmieri, with love, and in memory of the season "when grape leaves curl up like the hands of little dying grandmothers."

Milo March is a hard-drinking, womanizing, wisecracking, James-Bondian character. He always comes out on top through a combination of personality, bluff, bravado, luck, skill, experience, and intellect. He is a shrewd judge of human character, a crack shot, and a deeper character than I have found in most of the other spy/thriller novels I've read. But, above all, he is a con-man—and a very good one. It is Milo March himself who makes the series worth reading.

—Don Miller, *The Mystery Nook* fanzine 12

Steeger Books is proud to reissue twenty-three vintage novels and stories by M.E. Chaber, whose Milo March Mysteries deliver mile-a-minute action and breezily readable entertainment for thriller buffs.

Milo is an Insurance Investigator who takes on the tough cases. Organized crime, grand theft, arson, suspicious disappearances, murders, and millions and millions of dollars—whatever it is, Milo is just the man for the job. Or even the only man for it.

During World War II, Milo was assigned to the OSS and later the CIA. Now in the Army Reserves, with the rank of Major, he is recalled for special jobs behind the Iron Curtain. As an agent, he chops necks, trusses men like chickens to steal their uniforms, shoots point blank at secret police—yet shows compassion to an agent from the other side.

Whatever Milo does, he knows how to do it right. When the work is completed, he returns to his favorite things: women, booze, and good food, more or less in that order....

THE MILO MARCH MYSTERIES

CONTENTS

My name is Milo March. I'm an insurance investigator. It's not quite the same as being a private eye, even though I wear a trench coat, sometimes play a case by ear, and have been known to chase a blonde—when there wasn't a brunette around.

I have my own office on Madison Avenue—the martini capital of the United States. March's Insurance Service Corporation. I work for any of the insurance companies that wants to hire me. It means that I get most of the cases—life, fire, jewelry, or other valuables—which are too big or too hard for their regular claims departments. It's a living.

It had been three or four weeks since I'd been on a case and my bank roll was beginning to look as if it had taken a course at Slenderella. My fees were pretty high but the money didn't last long after I got through paying for my apartment and my office and supporting five or six of the leading bartenders in New York. I was trying to think of a way of drumming up a little business when the phone rang.

I picked up the receiver. "March's Insurance Service Corporation," I said in a voice which I hoped would convey the idea that I was so busy I could barely squeeze in one more case.

"Milo," a sexy contralto voice said, "have you really become as stuffy as you sound?"

I recognized the voice. It belonged to Merry Mellany. She was beautiful and blond and either the third or the fourth richest woman in the world. I could never remember which. I had worked on a case involving her jewels a couple of years earlier and we'd been friends ever since. And I mean just friends. It had just missed developing into something else several times. Sometimes I suspected the only reason it hadn't was that the thought of all that money scared me.

"I am not stuffy," I said indignantly. "But once in a while I have to sound as if this were an office and not an after-hours club. How are you, Merry?"

"Wonderful, but bored," she said. "Take me to lunch?"

"It's the best offer I've had all morning," I said. "Twelve-thirty at Cherio's?"

"Love you," she said. "I'll be there." She hung up.

I replaced the receiver, wondering why it always seemed so much easier to spend money than to make it. That seemed to be the only result of a hard money policy.

I had no sooner put the receiver down than the phone rang again. I picked it up and said, "Yeah?" I was back to normalcy.

"Milo?" It was a man's voice. It sounded like someone I knew.

"Yeah," I said again. It was a good line and I might as well stick with it until I got close enough to read the score.

"This is Martin Raymond," he said. I knew him, all right. He was a vice-president of Intercontinental Insurance, a company I'd done a lot of work for. "Got a minute?"

"I did a while ago," I said, "so it must be around here somewhere."

He rewarded me with a conference-room laugh. "That's my boy," he said. "Always making with the old boffola. Want to run over here? We have a problem maybe you and I can kick into shape."

"Let's just run it up a flagpole and see who salutes it," I said. "I'll be right over."

I hung up and looked at my watch. It was eleven o'clock. I called my answering service and told them I wouldn't be back until after two. Then I went out and walked up Madison Avenue.

Intercontinental had been one of the first insurance companies to move uptown. They had their own building on upper Madison. It was an imposing edifice of glass and steel, giving mute testimony to the profits in premiums. Up on Raymond's floor there was a redheaded receptionist who gave ample proof that they didn't think only of money. She checked on her phone and told me I could go in.

Raymond's office, on the other hand, was a triumph of cash over taste. Only slightly smaller than Grand Central Station, it was furnished in Early American, including a refurbished and glorified cobbler's bench that now held only a couple of ashtrays. The walls were covered with photographs of the early executives of Intercontinental, all of them looking like bandits who had come down out of the hills in their Sunday finery to have their pictures taken. Raymond was sitting behind a low table-desk, the top of which was bare except for a gold pencil and pad. The clean-desk bit was fashionable on Madison Avenue and was supposed to hint that here was a man so busy that he kept up with his work.

"Milo, boy, it's good to see you," he said as I came in. He waved a hand toward something that had once been an Early American cupboard and was now a bar. "I guess it's too early to offer you a drink."

"It's never too early," I said, "but I'll bear up without one. Somebody has to show those A.A.'s they're not the only ones who can keep a grip on themselves."

He laughed politely. "Want to go to work?"

"I never want to," I said, "but I like the money. It comes in handy when I want to add to my stamp collection. What's the job?"

"Just a small problem," he said. Which meant it was a tough one. "The name Dr. Jaime Moreno do anything to you?"

"Not especially," I admitted. "It's vaguely familiar, but that's all."

"He was a professor here at New York University. Vanished not long ago."

Then I remembered. Dr. Jaime Moreno had been a political refugee from one of the Latin American countries in the Caribbean. He'd been teaching Latin American literature at the university. He had left the university one evening and that was the last ever seen of him.

"I remember," I said. "He came from one of those banana republics in Central America."

"Sugar, not bananas," Raymond said. "He was an exile from the Monican Republic, or Republic of Santa Monica. He was pretty well known as a critic of the regime down there."

I was remembering more and that was putting it mildly. The Monican Republic was the personal property of a guy who called himself Generalissimo Francisco Torcido, or sometimes simply The Benefactor. He'd been the dictator of the country for the past thirty years, and according to all reports it had been one of the bloodiest rules in the world. The Monican Republic was a little country about the size of Illinois, bounded by the Dominican Republic, the Republic of Haiti, and the Caribbean.

"I remember reading about it in the papers," I said. "They never found him, huh?"

Raymond shook his head. "Not a trace."

"The theory," I said, "was that Torcido had him killed, wasn't it?"

"There are two theories," Raymond said carefully. "Moreno was the treasurer of some refugee fund amounting to about one hundred and thirty thousand dollars. The day after he 'vanished,' he showed up at the bank and drew all of the money out. That was the last time he was seen. So one theory is that he took the money and went to greener pastures. The other theory is that Generalissimo Torcido had him kidnapped and brought back down there, where he was killed. There is also the death of an American which some people are trying to tie in with it."

I remembered reading something about that. It had to do with an American pilot who had supposedly flown Moreno to the Monican Republic and then he, too, had vanished there. But I didn't ask any questions. I could always check it with someone who wasn't so careful as Raymond.

"After all," Raymond added irrelevantly, "the Monican Republic, while small, is an important member of the anti-Communist bloc, and Generalissimo Torcido is, I believe, well liked in Washington."

"Sure," I said, "and I remember hearing somewhere that Lucky Luciano helped us to win the war. Bedfellows make strange politics."

"Well," he said vaguely. He wasn't going to pursue that line. "In the meantime, everyone has been searching for Dr. Moreno. The New York police, the FBI, and a private group mostly composed of other refugees. There has been some prodding on the matter from Congress. Most recently, the Monican Republic has hired a couple of well-known lawyers and an investigator here in America to try to solve the mystery. I understand that the tourist business has fallen off since the incident and Torcido himself is anxious to have the matter cleared up."

"I'll bet," I said. I looked at him. "Do I get the impression that after all these people have failed to find the professor, you want me to step in and dig him up?"

"Not exactly," he said. "We carried no insurance on the man. I doubt if he had any. Under the circumstances, I suppose premiums would have been pretty high. No, we'd like you to find his manuscript."

"You lost me somewhere back there," I said.

"Dr. Moreno had just completed the manuscript of a book about the Torcido regime. In fact, except for minor revisions, he had completed it just a month before his disappearance. The only copy of the manuscript vanished with him."

"And you had insured it?"

He nodded unhappily. "For seventy-five thousand dollars.

The policy was to cover it for the six months before it would be published. The premium was substantial, but even so, it represents a considerable loss. Mrs. Moreno has just put in a claim for the money."

"And unless you can turn up the manuscript for her, you've got to pay off?"

"Precisely," he said. "Unfortunately, with the possible exception of the refugee group, no one else is looking for the manuscript. They are concentrating only on finding Dr. Moreno—and with no success to date."

"Heartless of them," I said. "Okay, you want the manuscript back. How far do you want me to go to get it back?"

"We want it," he said flatly.

"Suppose," I said, "that the one theory is right and it was the Generalissimo, brave anti-Communist and staunch ally that he is, who put the snatch on the professor and his book. That will mean that I have to go to the Monican Republic and try to pry it right out of the lion's mouth. What kind of premium would I have to pay if I wanted to take out a little extra life insurance before I go?"

"The rate would be pretty high," he admitted cautiously.

I grinned at him. "A small problem," I said. "What's the name of this lost opus?"

"The Bloody Reign of Torcido."

"Catchy title," I said. "Okay, Martin, I'll take it on. The usual one hundred a day and expenses."

He nodded, looking relieved. "I said you were the only man for it and I knew you'd pull it off."

"Relax, buster. If Torcido took it, it may be burned up by

now. And if that's the way the cookie crumbles, you'll have to pay off."

He winced. "We are aware of that. But if it's possible to recover it, we feel confident that you'll do it, Milo. Now, what do you want? The policy file?"

I shook my head. I doubted if there would be anything in it that would be any good to me. I'd have to dig up all of my own information. "Just the address and phone number of Mrs. Moreno," I said, "and five hundred dollars to cover expenses. If I have to go down there, I'll be drawing more."

He nodded and leaned over his desk, putting one hand in under it. "Get five hundred dollars from the cashier," he said, "and bring it in here. Charged to the Moreno case. And bring Mrs. Moreno's address and phone number." He was talking into a camouflaged intercom in the desk. I grinned to myself. Some Early American craftsman was probably spinning rapidly in his grave.

"The girl will have it here in a minute," he told me. "When will you start on this, Milo?"

"Right away," I said. "As soon as you give me the money, I'm going to take a beautiful girl to lunch and have an infinite number of dry martinis, all of which will put me in the right mood for the job. One doesn't attack a whole country without the aid of a little liquid courage."

He gave out with another of those Ivy League laughs. "That's my boy. Always making with the jokes. It's a good thing that I know you always deliver or I might take you seriously."

"You mean," I said, "it's a good thing I don't have to break down my expense account so that it shows every martini. You want interim reports or just one when I'm finished?"

"When you're finished, boy. We have every confidence in you."

The door opened and a pretty little blonde came in, carrying a small sheaf of bills and a slip of paper. She was a different secretary than had been there the last time I was hired. He seemed to use up secretaries faster than some men did scratch pads. I wondered if he wore them out chasing them around the Early American furniture.

He waited until she'd left and then shoved all of it toward me. "Here you are, Milo," he said.

I looked at the paper first. It had Mrs. Moreno's name, address, and phone number. Then I counted the money. There were ten fifty-dollar bills.

"Pretty," I said. "My favorite vitamin."

"Okay, boy," he said. "I'm glad you're on the team. I'll tell the Board of Directors to relax."

"You do that," I told him. I stood up. "If there's anything I can't stand it's a nervous Board member. I'll see you around." I stuffed the money in my pocket and left.

Merry was already sitting at the bar when I arrived at the restaurant. She hadn't been there long; her drink was barely started. I slipped onto the stool next to her and she leaned over for me to kiss her. I did.

"It seems to me that you get more beautiful every time I see you," I told her. "A dry martini," I added as the bartender came over.

"Who gets more beautiful?" she asked. "Me or the martini?"

"You. Martinis aren't beautiful. They're dry."

"I'm dry," she said promptly.

"I've noticed," I said. I looked at her again. "It's months since I've seen you. Which one of your houses are you living in at the moment—California, Texas, Florida, or Connecticut?"

"At the very moment, the St. Regis," she said, "but I'm going to Connecticut tomorrow. I thought maybe you might like to come up for the weekend."

"I'd love to, but I have to work."

She made a face. "You always have to work. Especially when I invite you somewhere."

The bartender brought my drink. It tasted like manna from heaven. "We can't all have a lapful of oil wells, honey."

"Why not?" she asked promptly. "Let me see, you and Greta are divorced by now, aren't you?"*

I nodded.

"Then all you have to do is marry me and you'll have a lapful of oil wells, too."

"It's a nice offer," I said, "but you know me. All that money would scare me. I'd be awakened every morning by the rustling of all those dollar bills. But I appreciate the offer just the same."

She sighed. "Well, I tried. I've never been able to seduce you by illicit means, so I thought I'd offer to make an honest man of you."

"An impossible task," I admitted. A vague idea was flitting around in the back of my head. "But there might be something you can do for me."

* In *As Old as Cain* (1954) Milo had married a young woman, Greta Brooks, whom he had met in East Germany in *No Grave for March* (1952). (All footnotes were added by the editor.)

She finished her drink, and as she put down the empty glass, the bartender had another drink for her. "What, darling?" she asked.

"First tell the bartender that I don't like to wait between drinks either." Just to demonstrate, I finished my drink. To my surprise, the bartender did have one there immediately. "Well, what do you know? Did you arrange all this before I came in? Or is this just another example of the power of money?"

"It has its advantages," she admitted. "What can I do for you?"

"I'm not sure," I said. "But this job I'm on may take me to the Monican Republic. If so, it would be better if I didn't go as an insurance investigator. Maybe I can cook up some sort of errand that I'm supposed to be doing for you."

"Anything," she said. "Not only that, but I'll go with you."

"No," I said firmly. "It's apt to be dangerous. I have enough trouble looking after myself without having to look after you too."

"You do love me," she said. "You just said you'd look after me."

"You're drunk," I said coldly. "All I said was that you can't go. And that's final."

"Yes, dear."

"How long will you be in Connecticut?" I asked.

"Two or three months, I suppose. Unless I get bored. How long will you be down there?"

"Not that long. Maybe I'll take you up on the weekend invitation when I come back. Anyway, if I do go and I decide to say I'm working for you, I'll call and tell you."

"That's a promise," she said.

We had a few more drinks and then we went upstairs and had lunch. It had been several months since I'd seen her and it was fun. After lunch I dropped her at the hotel and took the cab back to my office.

I let the answering service know that I was back and then I sat down to worry about the case. I'd see Mrs. Moreno later, but first I needed to get a thorough briefing. I had thought of going over to the public library and looking up the newspaper stories, but there would still be things missing from them. I needed a report from the inside. I pulled the phone over and called somebody I know on the police. I told him that I wanted the name of the man who had worked on the Moreno case. He promised to call me back.

It didn't take him more than fifteen minutes. "Johnny Rockland of the Bureau of Special Services and Investigation," he said. "Lieutenant. You want a letter of introduction or something?"

"For once I'm in luck," I said. "I know Johnny myself. Thanks."

I hung up and then I dialed again. I asked for Lieutenant Rockland and he was on a minute later. I told him I wanted to come down and talk to him about a case. He said he was busy at the moment, but that he could see me in about an hour. I promised I'd be there and hung up.

The phone rang again. A girl said it was Mr. Martin Raymond calling.

"Milo," he said when he came on, "how's it going?"

"Let me see," I said. "I've had the case for about two and a half hours. Don't you think you ought to give me another hour or so? Or is Intercontinental on an economy wave?"

"Just kidding you, boy," he said. "You may be getting some help soon."

"How?"

"Someone with a Spanish accent called here just a few minutes ago and wanted to know if we were interested in information about Jaime Moreno. The call was put through to me and I told him you represented us on the matter and to get in touch with you. You ought to be hearing from him soon."

"Big of you," I said. I wasn't exactly thrilled. "Tell me, has this Good Samaritan called before?"

"I don't know. Why?"

"Find out," I said.

"Hold on," he said. He cut off and I waited, drumming on the desk and hoping I was wrong. He was back shortly. "It may not have been the same man," he said, "but someone with a Spanish accent has called a couple of times to ask if we were interested in Moreno."

"Great," I said. I had a few choice thoughts about vice-presidents but I kept them to myself. "The next time somebody wants to do us a good turn, just get his name and phone number instead of giving him mine."

"What's wrong?" he asked.

"You just told someone that you're working on the case and you also told them who will be doing the work. If I get shot in the back, the bullet will have your initials on it."

"Nonsense," he said. "Besides, we have nothing to hide."

"Maybe you don't," I said, "but I do. Oh, I know that you

think a man can't be the head of a nice little republic like that and do such terrible things, but I want you to stop pretending he's a fellow club member and think of him as a gangster. That neck you stick out so confidently is mine."

"All right," he said stiffly.

"And good-bye," I added. When I'd hung up I expressed my opinion of vice-presidents out loud. That made me feel a little better. I got up and started to leave. I had just reached the door when the phone rang. I went back and picked it up.

"Yeah?" I said.

"Señor March?" a voice asked. It was a man's voice, but soft and silky, almost a whisper.

"Yeah."

"You are a private investigator, yes?" he asked. He spoke with a strong Spanish accent.

"I'm a private investigator, no," I said. "I'm an insurance investigator. You have the wrong man." But I was afraid that he didn't.

"No, no," he said. "You are the man we were told is very good."

"Who's we?" I asked.

"I represent someone who wishes an investigation done."

"Who is someone?"

"A most important man. I do not say at the moment."

"What kind of an investigation?"

"It is of a political nature."

"How interesting," I said. "We might make more progress if you provided more information. Exactly what kind of a job, when it's to be done, where it's to be done. Little things like that."

"It would mean going to Mexico," he said. "You would start at once. You would be gone perhaps three or four weeks. We would pay you two hundred dollars per day and your expenses."

"That's real neighborly of you," I said. "But I'm afraid I'll have to turn it down. I'm already working on a job."

"I know," he said. "We could pay you more, perhaps, if my offer was too low."

"No, thanks," I said. "I make it a rule to never work on two jobs at once. All work and no play makes Milo a bored boy."

There was a moment of silence. When he spoke again, his voice was even softer. "Señor March, it would not be wise of you to try to find Jaime Moreno."

"Yo caigo en ello," I said. "You mean you don't want me to find Moreno. Why didn't you say so in the beginning?" I wondered if the way he had phrased his sentence meant that he didn't know that I was only supposed to find a manuscript.

"If you agree to forget about it," he said, "then we will pay you five thousand dollars."

"So much?" I said. "That's a lot of money for a *chulo* to pay out."

There was another moment of silence. "You mean you will not accept it? Is that it, Señor?"

"You're a bright boy," I told him.

"You are not being wise, Señor," he said. "If you refuse to be paid in gold, you may have to take payment in another metal."

"Like lead?"

"Perhaps."

"Who'll make that payment?" I asked. "You, too?"

"Perhaps."

"Do you have a name?" I asked. "Or are you afraid to announce it?"

"I am sometimes known as El Nariz."

It didn't mean anything to me, although he'd announced it as if it were famous. *El Nariz* meant "The Nose," but that was all, as far as I was concerned.

"Never heard of you," I said. "Are you another *chulo?*"

"I am known as a man who keeps his word and shoots straight." He sounded as if he was getting angry.

"And I," I said, "am known as a man who lies like hell and shoots even straighter. If you are called El Nariz, it must mean that at least one part of you makes a good target. Maybe you'd better go to Mexico on that other job."

"Está bien," he said. "I will see you soon, Señor." There was a click as he hung up.

TWO

When I'd replaced the phone I relieved myself of some more of my feelings about vice-presidents. There was no question that the man who had just threatened me was the one to whom Martin Raymond had obligingly handed my name and phone number. It wasn't the threat that bothered me; it was that now they would know why I was there, if I had to go to the Monican Republic. I'd still use some sort of cover, but they'd know.

I started to leave, then went back and buckled on my shoulder holster. I took a .32 from the desk drawer and slipped it into the holster. I didn't often carry a gun, but the way El Nariz had sounded, it suddenly seemed like a good idea. Then I went out and took a cab downtown to Centre Street.

The Bureau of Special Services and Investigation is one branch of the police department which even New Yorkers know little about.* They work without publicity or public credit. Nearly everyone on the squad speaks several languages. They do almost everything, from guarding important foreign visitors to work on strikes and such things as the disappearance of Dr. Moreno. Johnny Rockland was a hell of a good cop who had been in the bureau for several years. I'd

---

* Anthony Bouza has written about this secretive unit of the NYPD, which is now called the Intelligence Division.

worked with him three or four times. He was a tall, well-built man in his early forties who looked more like a successful businessman than a cop. He looked up and grinned as I came into his office.

"Hi, Milo," he said. "How's the insurance business?"

"Like always," I said. "How are you, Johnny?"

"Busy—like always," he said. He looked me over. "I see you're on a new case. Must be a big one, too."

"What gave you that idea?"

"You're here, for one thing. You wouldn't come all the way downtown just to look into my big blue eyes. So it means you want to pick my brains. It must be big because you're wearing a gun. Your coat is well cut—better than a poor cop could afford—but there's still a little bulge."

"Don't tell me all the cops are making like Sherlock Holmes these days," I said. "What some people won't do to try to draw attention to themselves. Yeah, I'm working. The Moreno case."

"So?" he said. "I should've guessed that, too, since it's been my big headache for longer than I like to think. Somebody have some insurance on him and decided the cops won't ever solve it?"

I shook my head. "None on him. But Intercontinental insured the book he wrote. I guess they're afraid that everybody's so busy looking for the man, no one will think about the manuscript. So that's what I'm after. Johnny, who is El Nariz?"

"So that's the reason for the gun?" he said. "Where'd you run into him?"

"I didn't—yet. He phoned me just before I came down here. Offered me a job first, then five grand if I wouldn't have anything to do with the Moreno case. I called him a name when I refused and he didn't seem too friendly after that."

"How'd he know you were working on it?"

"He'd been calling up Intercontinental every few days and asking them if they were interested in information about Moreno. They just decided to do something about the manuscript and hired me today. He called again today and some jerk gave him my name and phone number. Who is he?"

"I don't know."

"Who're you kidding?" I demanded.

"It's true, Milo," he said. "I know a lot about him, but I've never seen him and I've never talked to anyone who's seen him. Even the Monican refugees here don't know who he is. I know that he's the chief assassin for the Monican regime, but I can't prove that. I know, but also can't prove, that he's killed six or seven people right here in New York City. I'm pretty sure that he's the one who kidnapped Dr. Moreno. Now that you tell me he's back in the city, he's probably the one who took a shot last night at another one of the refugees. Oh, I know a lot about him, but I can't prove any of it. The man himself is just a whisper."

"Sounds like quite a character," I said. "Does he live here?"

"I don't think so. The whisper is that he lives in Puerto Torcido and slips in and out of the United States whenever there's a killing to be done. We've fixed all sorts of traps, so he must come in illegally. I think I even know how."

"How?" I asked.

"Ever hear of Raimundo Perrola?"

I nodded. I'd heard of him, all right. So had anyone who had ever read the newspapers. He was a Monican diplomat, but that wasn't what he was famous for; it was for getting married. He'd been married five times, twice to two of the richest women in the world. The other three hadn't been exactly poor either. None of them had lasted long and he'd always ended up with a settlement.

"Well," he said, "every time there's been a Monican refugee killed here, Perrola has been around. He was in the city when Moreno disappeared. He's here now. He usually comes and goes in his own private plane. It's my idea that he brings El Nariz and bird-dogs the kill for him. But again, I can't prove it."

"Have you questioned Perrola?" I asked.

"He has diplomatic immunity and you can be sure he never waives it, not even for a speeding ticket."

"What else have you done about trying to locate El Nariz?"

"Everything under the sun," he said. "We've even asked the Chief of Police in Puerto Torcido about him. The Chief claims the name is not known there. The Monican refugees have some contacts there and have tried to find out through them. Nothing. As I told you, he is only a whisper."

"A pretty active one," I said dryly. "What about the Moreno case?"

He gave me a disgusted look. "Dr. Jaime Moreno was a very outspoken critic of Torcido. Has been ever since he came here five years ago. He was shot at a couple of times, so we've occasionally kept an eye on him. He belonged to the Monican Democratic Society, like most of the other refugees here. They try to guard each other, too. He taught at New York University uptown. They claim that he was threatened more after it was announced that he'd written a book about Torcido. Anyway, that night he was seen taking the subway. Alone. But he never arrived home."

"What about his being seen the next day?" I asked.

Johnny Rockland nodded. "Yeah, he was seen. He was the treasurer of a refugee fund. There was a hundred and thirty thousand in the account. Dr. Moreno appeared at the bank the following morning and drew it all out. There was another man with him. They walked out of the bank and there the trail ended."

"What about the other man?"

"We showed the teller some pictures. He thinks the other man was Perrola, but he's not positive. The teller also said that Dr. Moreno acted rather strangely. From his description, we think he was drugged. The refugee group declares that Moreno would never have taken the money for his own use."

"Was he bonded?"

"Yes. Littleton Bonding and Fidelity. But I know they haven't turned up anything either. So far as we can prove, the trail ended the minute he reached the sidewalk."

"What do you mean, so far as you can prove?" I asked.

"That afternoon," he said, "an American pilot named Mike Dayton with a chartered plane took off from a New Jersey airport. He carried one passenger, who was supposed to be a sick man from New York City. The passenger was taken onto the plane in a stretcher. The plane stopped in Miami and took on more gas and then flew to Puerto Torcido."

"Interesting," I said.

"It gets more so," he said. "We haven't been able to trace the sick man back here. We've asked Puerto Torcido about him and gotten no answer. A few days after making the trip, the American pilot was killed in Puerto Torcido. Supposedly in a personal fight. The man who killed him, Alberto de la Garra, was arrested and two days later committed suicide in his cell in Puerto Torcido."

"All tied up," I said.

"Gift-wrapped," he grunted. "When the Generalissimo was questioned about Moreno, he said it was a problem of the New York City police. More recently he's hired some people here to solve the case just to prove that he's innocent. But you can be sure that he had everything concealed before he hired them. For my money, Milo, Dr. Moreno, alive or dead, is in the Monican Republic. And so is his book."

"You're probably right," I said. "Well, I guess it'll mean a little trip for me."

"You're going there?"

"If that's where the trail leads."

"Okay," he said. "Do me a little favor. While you're looking for the book, keep one eye out for the man. And let me know anything you dig up. Maybe I can't do anything with it except keep it as a souvenir, but I'd like to know it anyway."

"Sure," I said. "Anything else on it?"

"That's about it," he said. "When will you leave?"

"Not for a day or two. There are a few things I want to do. And I want to talk to Mrs. Moreno and maybe some of the other refugees. Maybe I can even use some of their contacts down there if it becomes necessary."

"I doubt it. The few people who are still in the country and still opposed to Torcido have to be pretty quiet. But you might get something. Right now I understand that at least two of the refugee group are staying with Mrs. Moreno all the time. When are you going to see her?"

I looked at my watch. The afternoon was pretty well gone. "Maybe this evening," I said. "If she'll see me then."

"They're being pretty careful," he said. "Maybe I'd better give you a little help."

He pulled his phone over and dialed a number. After a minute, he said, "This is Lieutenant Rockland. Will you call me back?" Then he hung up.

"What was that for?" I asked.

"I told you they're being careful. They won't talk unless they're certain it's me, and the only way they can be sure is when they call me themselves."

The phone rang. He picked up the receiver and said hello. Then he told whoever was on the other end about me and that I wanted to talk to them. He listened for a minute, then said, "Fine. Then he'll be there at about eight tonight. Yes, I'll tell him. Good-bye." He hung up and looked at me. "They'll expect you. You speak Spanish, don't you?"

"Yeah," I said.

"They all speak English, but you'll probably need the Spanish when you get down there. In the meantime, when you go there tonight, there's a sentence to identify yourself with."

"What?"

"Dichosos los ojos que ven a usted."

"Happy are the eyes that see you," I repeated. "What's the idea?"

He shrugged. "Just a password. Okay, good luck, Milo. Let me know if there's anything I can do."

"Thanks, Johnny."

"And if you do run into El Nariz," he said, "you'd better be quick with that gun, boy. And pull the trigger once for me."

I said I would and left. I took a cab up to the Village and got out at Sheridan Square. I bought a paper, then walked down to the Blue Mill Tavern on Commerce Street. I said hello to Victor, Manuel, and Alcino behind the bar, and Alcino started making a dry martini without being told. It was one of the few places in the Village where the martinis were good.

I had three martinis at the bar, drinking them slowly and admiring the hostess as she walked around. Then I took a table and had a leisurely dinner. Afterwards I had a brandy with my coffee, and by the time I'd finished that, it was time to go.

Mrs. Moreno lived over by Washington Square. I walked through Waverly Place to the Square and then started searching for her number. I found it and pressed the bell beneath her name. The buzzer answered and I went in and walked up the two flights. I pressed another button beside the door.

The door opened a bare three inches and a man looked out. He was small and dark with a hunted look in his eyes.

"Yes?" he asked.

"Dichosos los ojos que ven a usted," I said, feeling like a character in a spy novel.

"Señor March?" he asked.

"Yes," I said.

"From the insurance company?"

"Yes."

He opened the door wider. "Please come in."

I stepped inside. He closed the door and bolted it and then turned to me. "You must pardon all this," he said with a tight little smile, "but we have learned to be careful. I am Federico Laragoza. I was a very good friend of Dr. Moreno's."

We shook hands.

"Come this way," he said. He led the way through the apartment to another room. In it was another man, a big, beetle-browed man, and a little woman with a beautiful dark face beneath white hair.

"Señora Moreno," the first man said, "this is Señor March from the insurance company. And Señor Alejandro Goma, another friend of Dr. Moreno."

They both murmured something and I shook hands with the second man.

"May we offer you some brandy, Señor March?" the woman asked. She smiled. "It was always Jaime's favorite after dinner."

"I'd like it, thank you," I said.

"Would you serve it, Federico?" she asked.

The little man went out of the room and came back with a bottle of brandy and glasses. He poured the brandy and handed around the glasses.

"To success," I said, lifting my glass. We all drank. "Señora," I said then, "I believe you know I am from the Intercontinental Insurance Company and I am here because of the insurance on your husband's book."

"I do not care about the book," she said. "That is, I do not really care about the money that was to be paid if it were lost. But no one seems to do anything about finding Jaime, and we thought perhaps if you were looking for the book you might find him. It is Jaime that I want back."

"I understand," I said.

"It was, in fact, my suggestion," the smaller man said. "If Dr. Moreno was taken to our country, as we think, the police of course can do nothing about following. But it occurred to me that there would be no such restrictions on insurance detectives. So I suggested that the insurance money be asked for and perhaps that would make the insurance company do something. You see, we are being frank with you."

"I appreciate that," I said. "You understand that I must go looking for the manuscript. If, however, I should also see the man, I will not ignore him."

"We can ask for no more," he said with a sigh. "Of course, it would be nice if both Dr. Moreno and the manuscript could be rescued. The book would do much to show Americans what Torcido is really like. It was a beautiful job."

"You have seen it?" I asked.

He nodded.

"How large a manuscript was it?" I asked.

"The usual size sheets of paper. I believe there were about four hundred pages. But why, Señor?"

"Just curious," I said. "You feel certain that both Dr. Moreno and the manuscript are already in the Monican Republic?"

"Yes."

"If what you say about the Monican ruler is true," I said,

"then doesn't it seem logical to assume—you will forgive me, Señora—that Dr. Moreno is no longer alive?"

"Perhaps," he said. "There is, however, a small chance that he might be in prison. Torcido has sometimes kept his enemies as prisoners for a long time before killing them."

"Wouldn't he also destroy the manuscript?"

"He wouldn't, but it may have been destroyed. It would depend. You see, Señor, Torcido has ruled so long and his men know his methods so well that it is not always necessary for him to tell them to do a thing. It is said that Torcido himself, now that he is older, would prefer to have less bloodshed. Perhaps this is so and he does not always know what has been done until afterwards. If this should be true, perhaps one of his men would destroy the manuscript. If it reached Torcido, however, he would keep it. He has a room in the Palace where he keeps all sorts of things as souvenirs. I think he would keep it there as a reminder of his own power."

"I see," I said. "Do you know El Nariz?"

"We know El Nariz, Señor," he said softly. "Why do you ask?"

"Just curious," I said. "He phoned me earlier."

"Es un mal bicho," the bigger man said suddenly. It was the first time he had spoken. "Perhaps the Señor knows this since he is ready."

"Ready?" I asked.

"He means you are carrying a gun," the smaller man said. "It is well to be armed around El Nariz."

"Who do you think he is?"

He shrugged. "We do not know. We have tried to learn, for

we are sure that he is the killer who is always sent after us. Perhaps the Lieutenant told you that we are certain it was he who kidnapped Dr. Moreno. But we know nothing about him. You know more than we, for you have talked to him; those of us who may have talked to him are now dead."

"What about the hundred and thirty thousand dollars?" I asked.

They exchanged glances. "We can only tell you," the woman said gently, "that Jaime would never have touched a penny of that money for himself, not even if I were starving. That money was for those who fled our country and could not earn money at once; Jaime used to say that it was the blood line in the fight against Torcido."

"We can say more than that," the little man said. "We can say there was someone with Dr. Moreno when the money was withdrawn and that we are certain it was that Perrola, the scented one who runs and points Torcido's finger at those who are to be killed."

"Why talk?" the bigger man said. "We already know that this huge, powerful country can do nothing against such as he. We have seen our comrades die one by one and they do nothing. They will do nothing."

"Wait a minute," I said. "There are reasons why the police haven't done anything. Reasons which could be done away with, but if they were, then we would be no better than your Torcido. Freedom is not bought with counterfeit coins."

"You are right, Señor," the small man said. "We know you are right, but sometimes it is hard to remember when you see a friend die."

"Okay," I said, "I didn't mean to make a speech. We've got some counterfeiters here for that matter. Anyway, I'm going to your country soon. I am going to look for the book, but I will also look for the man who last had possession of it. If I find both, I will try to return with both."

"We cannot ask for more," the little man said. "Anyway I look at it," I said, "it's going to be a big order and I'm only one person. There may be times when I will need help there— maybe nothing more than information. This is where you can come in. Can you put me in touch with any of your people down there?"

The three of them exchanged glances again, but it was the little man who was the spokesman. "The few people down there who still fight are always in terrible danger," he said. "We have come to trust Lieutenant Rockland and he in turn seems to trust you. Still, we cannot take the responsibility of giving you the names of people. Many things might happen. But perhaps something can be done. Where will you be staying?"

"I don't know," I said. "What's the best hotel in Puerto Torcido?"

"The Torcido Hotel," he said with a wry grin. "All right. We will see that someone comes to see you there. He will identify himself to you with the same sentence you used in coming here and with his name. He will be a Señor Fulano."

I grinned. Señor Fulano is the same as saying, in English, Mr. So-and-So, or Mr. What's-his-name. "All right," I said. "That's fair enough. Anything else that you can tell me that will help?"

"I do not think so—except to be careful."

"That's one of the things I get paid for," I said. "I'll do whatever I can about Dr. Moreno. If he's alive, I'll try to get him out."

"Que Dios le oiga," the woman said fervently.

"I will go tomorrow or the day after," I said. "Tell your friend to get in touch with me then. Now, good night."

They all said good night and the small man escorted me to the door. There he said good night again as he let me out. I went down the stairs and out onto the street.

It was still early, but there was little traffic on the street. I looked around for a taxi. There was one parked about a block away. Its lights came on and it moved forward even before I could wave.

It rolled up to me slowly and stopped. I was about to reach for the door handle when something stopped me. I was never sure what, but I think it may have been the glint of the street-light on metal in the front seat. Without trying to find out what it was, I threw myself backwards and toward the rear of the cab. At the same moment, there was a streak of fire and the roar of a gun from the front seat. Somewhere behind me, glass shattered.

I hit the sidewalk rolling and then half rolled and half scrambled around behind the cab. There was another shot, and the bullet bounced off the sidewalk and screamed into the distance. Then I was behind the cab where he couldn't see me.

There was a deep growl from the motor and a thin screech from the tires as the cab leaped forward. It began picking up speed rapidly. I stayed where I was, lying in the gutter, and yanked my gun from its holster. I steadied my arm on the street and pulled the trigger slowly. I was aiming for the tires, and on the third shot I made it just before the cab reached the corner. It veered sharply as the tire exploded, then sunfished across the street as the driver wrestled with the wheel. It bounced off a fire hydrant and careened into a tree. The motor coughed into silence.

A moment later I heard the cab door open, but it was on the far side and I couldn't see the man. I stayed flat on my belly and waited. When I finally saw him, he was already across the street and was only a flicker in the shadows on MacDougal Street. I knew it was hopeless, but I still snapped a shot at him.

"Hasta luego, señor," a voice called. It was not much more than a whisper, but it carried to me clearly and I recognized it as the voice I'd heard on the phone. I still had my gun raised, but now there was nothing to see.

Somewhere back of me there was the sound of a window going up and the excited babble of voices. In the distance a siren suddenly wailed. I put my gun away and ran around the corner. A block away I found another cab. I got in and gave him my address. We drove away and the siren became fainter and fainter.

THREE

When we reached the street where I lived, I had the taxi stop at the corner. I didn't know if El Nariz was still gunning for me and I didn't think he knew where I lived, but I wasn't going to take any chances. I got out and stood on the corner until the cab pulled away. It was one of the little side streets in the Village and it was pretty deserted. I took out my gun and put fresh bullets in it. Then I put it back in the holster and made sure it was loose.

There were no cars coming, so I walked down the middle of the street watching the doorways on either side. I felt a little foolish, like an imitation of a cowboy in a cheap movie, but I also felt safer. When I reached my building, I cut across to it and went in.

Upstairs, I got out of my coat and poured myself a generous drink of rye on the rocks. I took out my little black book and looked up Johnny Rockland's home phone number. I went over to the phone and dialed it.

His wife answered in a weary voice. All cops' wives sound like that. Especially when they answer phones, because they know that every phone call may mean their husbands have to go out into the night no matter what they're doing. Maybe never to come back.

"I want to talk to Johnny," I told her. "Tell him it's Milo March."

He came on the phone a moment later. "Don't tell me you already have it solved," he said.

"I tried," I said. "About thirty minutes ago there was a shooting down by Washington Square. Nobody was hurt and both men escaped before the cops got there. The only casualty was a tire of a taxi, which then piled into a tree. The man who was driving the cab was El Nariz. I thought you might like to know."

"Nice of you," he said dryly. "I suppose I shouldn't ask who the second man was, just in case it's a friend of mine I'd have to pull in for questioning?"

"You can't expect me to know everything," I said. "In fact, there are a few things I'd still like to know."

"That figures," he said. "Sometimes I wonder whether the New York City Police Department works for the taxpayers or for Milo March. What do you want to know?"

"Only the things I thought you'd want to know too," I said piously. "Where'd the taxi come from? Maybe there will be fingerprints in it if you're lucky. Little things like that."

"Sure," he said. "Okay. Do you want to get off the phone so I can go to work, or must I be rude?"

"You'll call me?"

"I'll call you. Where are you? Home?"

"Yeah."

"Good-bye," he said and hung up.

I replaced the receiver and devoted myself to my drink and a few choice thoughts about El Nariz. It was a half hour before my phone rang. By that time I was well into my second drink. I scooped up the receiver.

"Yeah?" I said.

It was Johnny Rockland. "My wife hates you, too," he announced. "You've ruined a perfectly good thirty minutes of a bridge game. But you know, you were right. There was a gun fight down there."

"Imagine that."

"The taxi was stolen. It had been reported about two hours earlier. The local witnesses weren't any help at all. The I.D. boys haven't finished going over the cab yet. They say it's full of prints, but they don't think we'll get anything from them because the steering wheel is clean. Wiped clean. Two .32 automatic shells on the floor in the front of the cab. Won't mean a thing."

"Well, it was a good try," I said. "I got a theory. You want to hear it?"

"Go ahead."

"He made his try and missed," I said. "I don't think he'll try again—here. They'll expect me to go to the Monican Republic. In fact, that's probably the only reason he tried to get me—because I can go there, whereas the police can't. Now he'll go home and wait for me. So if you're right about how he comes and goes, this might be the time to start keeping an eye on Perrola."

"As much as I hate to admit it," he said, "maybe you do have an idea there. Get off the phone and let me do something about it."

I hung up and went back to my drinking. It was another thirty or forty minutes before the phone rang again. I picked it up on the first ring.

"It was a good idea, but too late," he said sourly. "Perrola took off in his personal plane two hours ago. Said he was heading home. Hasn't been heard from since."

"Two hours ago?" I said. "Damn. That must mean El Nariz is still hanging around."

"Not necessarily. In fact, I suspect you're right, Milo. But Perrola couldn't take El Nariz on as a passenger from Idlewild. Or bring him in there. What he could do is land at some small field, maybe in New Jersey, and wait. In that case, El Nariz would be on his way now. If not already there. It's almost two hours since he took a crack at you."

"So where does that leave us?"

"Probably right where we were," he said. "I've got the boys trying to check the small airports in New Jersey, but I don't expect anything from it. And I've asked the Miami police to check for unregistered aliens if Perrola lands there for additional gas. That's all I can do, and I don't think it'll mean anything."

"You're probably right," I said. "Tell your wife I'm sorry I busted up the evening."

"I never liked bridge anyway," he said. "Just play it to make her happy. I'll let you know tomorrow if we get anything on the prints. And, Milo—"

"Yeah?"

"The next time, try to shoot a little better," he said. "Good night."

I said good night and hung up. After that I had one more drink and then I went to bed.

I was up fairly early the following morning and working out the next steps while I had my coffee. When I'd finished the second cup, I got on the phone. Pan American told me it would take me nine hours to reach Puerto Torcido, changing planes at Miami. Knowing I needed a little time, I made a reservation on the flight for the next morning. Then I dug out the slip of paper and dialed Mrs. Moreno's number.

"Hello," a man's voice said cautiously.

"This is Milo March," I said. I remembered what Johnny Rockland had done the day before. "I want to ask you something, but if you'd like to make sure, you can call me back. I'm at home and the number is listed in the phone book. Do you want to do that?"

"*Sí, por cierto,*" he said.

I hung up and lit a cigarette while I waited. The phone rang almost immediately. I picked it up.

"Yeah?" I said.

"Señor March?"

"Yeah."

"Federico Laragoza here. You wished something?"

"You saw Moreno's manuscript?" I asked.

"Many times," he said. "He was kind enough to ask me to read it and to make suggestions."

"Good," I said. "How was it bound?"

"I do not understand," he said.

"The manuscript," I explained, "was it covered in any way? I want to know what sort of cover it had on it."

"*Claro que sí,*" he said. "It had a light blue cover. That is a single blue sheet on the front and one on the back. It was fastened together with little clasps running through holes punched in the paper. Is this what you wish, Señor?"

"Exactly," I said. "Anything written on the front cover?"

"Yes. The title of the book and Dr. Moreno's name."

"Thanks," I said. "I'll be seeing you."

"Señor," he said, "last night immediately after you left, there was a disturbance in the street …"

"There was a disturbance in the street," I admitted. "I was on one end of the disturbance and El Nariz was on the other. But don't worry. I was the one he was looking for. But by now he's probably gone home to wait for me."

"You are going?"

"Tomorrow."

"Cuidado," he said.

"I'll be careful," I told him. I thanked him again and hung up. I buckled on my holster and gun and shrugged into my coat. I went downstairs and took a cab to my office. The mail was on the floor, but there was nothing in it except bills. There were no messages. I told the girl to catch all the calls from now on until I told her differently. Then I phoned Intercontinental and asked for Martin Raymond.

"How are you this morning, Milo?" he asked, coming on.

"I'm just fine," I told him.

"By the way, did that informant get in touch with you?"

"Did you read your morning newspaper?" I asked.

"Yes."

"Did you happen to notice a little item about a mysterious gun battle down in Greenwich Village?"

"I believe I did notice it," he said.

"Well, that was your informant trying to give me what he had for me."

There was a moment of silence. "I'm sorry, Milo," he said then. "I just didn't realize—"

"You just didn't realize that Torcido was dangerous," I said. "Well, he is. So after this, if anyone calls up asking questions, tell them that I've been taken off the case. Tell them I spent too much money. Which reminds me, I'm going to the Monican Republic tomorrow."

"You're convinced the manuscript is there?"

"Yeah. And I'll need some money."

"Sure," he said without much enthusiasm. "How much, Milo?"

"Have them get a thousand dollars ready for me. I'll pick it up sometime today. For expenses."

"That will make fifteen hundred," he said. "Do you really need that much?" He didn't really care about money; at least, not any more than he did about his blood.

"They tell me those women down there are expensive," I said. "Besides, it's cheaper than paying out seventy-five grand. Don't worry, buster, if there's any change left over, I'll bring it back to you. And I'll make the girls give me receipts."

"Very well," he said stiffly. "The money will be here for you. What are your plans?"

"To spend the money," I said. "Good-bye." I hung up before he could answer. I went downstairs and hailed a cab. I told the driver to take me to Third Avenue.

In this business you meet a lot of people. Some of them are pretty unusual—and convenient at times. I was going to see a man who just about headed the list in both ways. His name was Allister Laird. He was an ex-con, having served a term for forgery some twenty years ago. When he came out he swore he would never spend another day in prison. He hadn't, although not for lack of people trying to put him there. He had a legitimate business, but the police department was full of men who declared that this was only a front for a much larger business. He always had a bunch of ex-cons working for him, and among them you could find some of the finest craftsmen the underworld had ever produced. But nothing had been pinned on him or his employees in twenty years.

Allister Laird had an antique store on Third Avenue. It was a big store, and back of it was a huge warehouse filled to the eaves with antiques. The warehouse also contained a carpentry shop and a well-equipped workroom. The store and warehouse were filled with genuine antiques of all kinds, ranging from rare manuscripts and coins through ancient armor up to very fine furniture. But if you wanted some special antique and he didn't have it, he'd make it for you in a few days. His craftsmen in the back could make a chair of Louis XIV or an old Spanish gold coin that would fool all but the best of the experts.

Some of the best homes on Park Avenue and up in Westchester County boasted Allister Laird's imitations and never knew it. But even then there was nothing the police could pin on him. His approach was exactly the same whether the piece in question was genuine or fake. "This," he would say, "appears to be an authentic Louis XIV, but I wouldn't know. I'm just a shopkeeper; if I like the looks of something, I pick it up, but I don't know if it's genuine or not. So, madam, I guarantee nothing."

In fact, that statement was part of the front of his shop. Just below the sign that said *Laird's Antiques,* there was a smaller sign which proclaimed: *I guarantee nothing.* Instead of driving customers away, it seemed to bring them in flocks.

Although no one had ever been able to prove it, it was true that Allister Laird did a thriving business in the small hours of the night in addition to what he sold in the day. Well-dressed, furtive men came to his door and departed with such things as authentic land deeds and important documents made to their order.

Some of Allister's success was probably due to his appearance. For a man dealing indiscriminately in the fake and the genuine, it was perfect. He was tall with the slight stoop of a man who has spent his life peering into murky corners. His clothes seemed to have been hung carelessly on his frame yet managed to impart a well-groomed air. His hair was prematurely white; since it was also luxurious and fluffy, he looked like a man with his head in a cloud. But his face was the gem, for it was the face of the innocent: unlined, shining with honesty, and appearing to have just been bathed in the milk of human kindness. Only people who were completely soured on life, like cops and insurance detectives, could ever believe such a man capable of wrong.

The taxi deposited me in front of the store and I went in. Allister was there, paying court to a pigeon-breasted woman who was looking at chairs. I went to the other end of the shop and examined some small statues while I waited.

The woman finally left and he came over. "Were you looking for something in the line of undraped female forms?" he asked gravely as if he'd never seen me before.

"I wouldn't mind," I said just as gravely, "but I'd prefer that they weren't antiques."

"I never guarantee the speed of a horse or the age of a woman," he said. He grinned at me. "It's nice of you, Milo, to come all the way across town to visit with an old man in his poor shop."

I grinned back at him. He knew damn well I wanted something. "I'm the friendly type," I said. "Is your warehouse still filled with junk?"

"Junk?" he said in a pained voice. "My dear young man, my warehouse contains nothing but the rarest of treasures from all over the world. What did you have in mind?"

"Something cheap," I said, "in an old Spanish manuscript. It wouldn't have to pass inspection by experts, but I'd like it to look fairly good."

"Let me see," he said. "I believe I have an original Cervantes somewhere."

I shook my head. "Something in the Americas if possible. The trouble is, I don't have time to wait for you to make one."

"You sound like a policeman," he said coldly. "As a matter of fact, I believe I do have something else, the remnant of an ill-starred venture that never materialized. The gentleman for whom it was intended has—er—retired."

"Sing Sing?"

"Something like that," he said. "I'll be right back, Milo." He went through the rear door that led to the warehouse.

I walked around, looking at things and waiting. There was an old chess set that had me interested until I saw the price on it. I'd pretty well covered the shop by the time the door opened and Allister came back in. He was carrying a manuscript that looked to be about the right size.

"You are in luck," he said. "Not only do I have such a manuscript but it turns out to be a rare one. An account of his voyage and landing in America by Christopher Columbus."

"By whom?" I asked.

"By Christopher Columbus. That's what it says on the manuscript. It seems to be even written in his own hand. See for yourself."

I took it from him. The cover on it made no attempt to be anything but modern, but the pages inside were properly aged; the Spanish was old and the writing faded.

"Very nice," I said. "Frankly, I'm not sure that Columbus could even write."

"A mere detail," he said loftily. "He probably learned on the way over. After all, he had lots of time."

"Well, it might do," I said doubtfully. "How much?"

"A bargain," he said promptly. "Only because you're my friend do I admit that it's something left over. A manuscript like this is easily worth several thousand dollars. But for you, my friend—one hundred dollars."

"Fifty," I said.

He looked pained. "Only a man with no soul would think of offering a paltry fifty dollars for a genuine Columbus."

"It's not even genuine Columbus, Ohio," I said. "Fifty."

"I am a man crucified upon the parsimony of my friends," he complained.

"Very well. I will not haggle."

I took fifty dollars from my pocket and gave it to him. "I'm already paying you twice what it's worth. Besides, knowing you, the original customer probably paid you for the job before he was thrown in the pokey."

"He did pay a small stipend," he admitted, "but that has nothing to do with it. Why, the craftsmanship alone in that manuscript is worth more than fifty dollars. Think of the art that went into it. Where could you find its equal?"

"It's good," I said. "Who did it?"

"Louie Perth," he said, naming one of the top forgers in the country.

"What did you pay him?"

"Well," he said slowly, "Louie owed me a small favor at the time …"

"I knew it," I said. "I should have offered you ten bucks for it."

"Just between old friends," he said with a grin, "I would have taken it."

"And I," I said, grinning back at him, "would have been willing to pay a hundred. Which should make us even. I'll see you around, Allister."

"Sure," he said.

I went out and took a cab across town to the Epicure. I ordered a martini and then went to the phone booth. It took several tries to locate Merry Mellany. She hadn't gone back to Connecticut yet, but was still at the hotel. They located her in the bar. I should have thought of trying it first.

"Milo," she said when she came on the phone, "are you calling to say you've changed your mind?"

"No," I said. "I've called to ask a favor."

"Anything," she said. "Including me."

"How many martinis have you had?" I asked suspiciously.

"Only four."

"Pig," I said. "I'm just having my first one. That's the trouble with you idle rich. I want to say that I'm working for you. Okay?"

"Okay. What are you doing?"

"You," I said, "have suddenly taken an interest in Early Americana. You have heard that there is a genuine Christopher Columbus manuscript somewhere in the Monican Republic and you have commissioned me to go find it."

"I have?" she said. "What the hell would I do with it if you found it?"

"Probably hang it in the bathroom just to show how rich you are," I said. "Or maybe give it to a museum. But don't worry. I won't find it. I just want that as an excuse for being there—not that anyone will really believe it."

"Okay," she said. "I wish you'd tell me what's going on."

"Nothing for your delicate ears," I told her. "Look, honey, this isn't a game like one of your companies opening a new oil well. Somebody may get hurt and it might even be me. I'm not quite sure what I'm doing. I'm going to have to play it as it comes up. If something happens and I call you from down there, just remember that the phone is probably tapped."

"All right, Milo," she said. "I'll take my cues from you."

"Good girl. And thanks, honey."

"When will I see you?" she asked.

"Probably when I get back," I said. "I won't know when that

will be until it happens. Take care, Merry."

"You take care," she said.

"Sure," I said and hung up. I went in and drank my martini. I ordered another one. I was still rushing the lunch hour a little, so I decided I had the time to try to slice myself a little more melon. I went back to the phone booth and looked up the number of the Littleton Bonding and Fidelity Company. I dialed the number and asked the operator for Ben Brackett. I'd worked for him a couple of times.

"Milo," he said when he came on, "how the hell are you? Haven't seen you in a century."

"Not since the last time," I admitted gravely. "How are things?"

"Same old grind," he said. "And you?"

"I'm living high on the hog," I said. "But you know how it is. I'd like to get higher. I hear that you're riding for a hundred and thirty grand loss on the Moreno case."

"Where'd you hear that?" he asked.

"The grapevine," I said. "You know I'm a great admirer of grapes. What have you done on it so far?"

"Just between us," he said, lowering his voice as if it were a party line, "not a thing. We haven't been able to get a lead."

"I'm interested in another angle of it," I said. "How would you like a fighting chance to find out where the money went for a hundred a day, no expenses?"

"You?"

"Me."

"What's the catch?" he asked.

"No catch," I said. "I have a job related to this. One that

doesn't involve finding the man or the money. You want to pay a hundred a day and no expenses, I'll look for money, too. If you don't, I'll stick to my knitting."

There was a moment of silence. "Okay," he said then. "It's a deal. But with a limit of fifteen days on it."

"When did I ever need fifteen days?" I said. "What's wrong? The company getting low on cash?"

"We just don't think there's too much chance of recovering," he said. "But we'll go up to fifteen hundred."

"Okay. Write me a letter confirming this. Starting as of today."

"Why today?"

"Because I'm already working on it. I'm leaving tomorrow for the Monican Republic."

"In that case, will do," he said. He sounded a little more enthusiastic. "I was afraid you were going to try to do it from Madison Avenue."

"The only thing that can be done on Madison Avenue," I said, "is dip for the olives in the martinis. And if you're caught, it means a demotion for not using lemon peel. I'll see you around, Ben."

"Sure," he said. "Call me when you get back and I'll buy you lunch as a bonus over the bill."

"Big of you," I said. I hung up and went back to my drink. Two martinis later I had lunch.

On my way back to my office, I stopped by Intercontinental and picked up the extra expense money. It made a comfortably warm spot in my pocket. Then I went to Pan American and got my ticket for the next day. I went on back to my office.

I spent an hour or so making sure that everything was cleaned up in the office.

There wasn't anything important, but I wasn't sure how long I'd be gone. I used a Dictaphone to get off some letters and then called the typing service and told them to pick up the tape. I checked with the phone service to make sure they had everything straight and understood that anything other than routine calls should be routed to my attorney. That was about it. I had a small drink from the bottle in my desk and was ready to go.

I had just stood up when I was aware that there was a shadow against the frosted glass in the door to my office. Not only that, but I could see it was a shapely shadow. It was going to be a pity, I thought, if I had to turn down a case like that. If it *was* a case, because whoever it was, she was just standing there and not making any effort to come in.

I cleared my throat but nothing happened. I turned the light off and on. Same result. I walked halfway across to the door, whistling loud enough to be heard on the other side. Finally I got some action. The shadow moved and there was a gentle knock on the door.

"Come in," I said.

The door opened and she came in. It was worth waiting for. She was small and built—well, as the boys in the backroom would say, like a well-known brick building. She had black hair, falling almost to her shoulders, and expressive black eyes. She was, to sum it up, quite a dish.

"Señor Milo March?" she asked. She had a soft Spanish accent.

I admitted that was who I was.

She was carrying a large, shiny black handbag. She opened it and peered in. She reached inside, and when her hand reappeared, it was holding a pastel blue gun. So help me. Real pastel blue. While maybe that made it look like a boudoir toy, the muzzle looked lethal and it was pointing straight at me.

"I have come to kill you," she said.

FOUR

A pretty girl doesn't walk into your office every day and threaten to kill you. It's a novelty as well as a threat. And this girl was very pretty. Hardly the type to go around killing. Even her little pastel blue gun was attractive if you forgot that it could shoot a bullet just as effectively as a less pretty one. Despite all the novelty, the girl seemed quite serious in what she was saying and the gun was steady. Too steady.

"Why?" I asked. It seemed like a reasonable question.

"You go to Puerto Torcido tomorrow?" she asked.

"Yes."

"That is why I kill you," she said. She sounded as if she thought it explained everything.

"New tourist policy?" I asked. "If so, it seems a little drastic to me."

"Do not make the jokes," she said. "I am going to kill you. You deserve it."

"Possibly," I admitted. "Do you mind if I have a last cigarette? I will smoke most carefully."

She hesitated as though uncertain. "All right," she said, "but you must make it quickly. And be most careful."

"*Sí, por cierto,*" I said. I reached slowly into my pocket and brought out my cigarettes and matches. I held them out. "Will you have one?"

"No, you must hurry, Señor." She sounded nervous.

"Surely," I said. I took a cigarette and lit it. I looked at her over the edge of it. "It is not often that a man is killed; it is even less often it is done by a beautiful girl. You remind me of something I once read. Do you know the name Juan Ruiz?"*

She didn't answer, but something in her expression told me that she did. I shifted to Spanish and started it as well as I could remember:

Quiero vos abreviar la predicación,

que siempre me pagué de pequeño sermón,

e de dueña pequeña et de breve razón,

ca lo poco e bien dicho finca en el corazón.

Del que mucho fabla rien, quien mucho ríe es loco;

es en la dueña chica amor grande e non poco;

dueñas hay muy grandes que por chicas non troco,

e las chicas por las grandes, non se arrepiente del troco.

De las chicas—

"Señor," she said. She sounded like she was about to crack.

"Sorry," I said. "I thought perhaps you liked poetry." I took another drag on the cigarette. Then, holding it between my thumb and middle finger, I flicked it into her open handbag. She gasped and looked down.

I stepped in quickly and put my hand over her hand and the gun, pushing it to one side. I tried to squeeze down hard enough so that she couldn't fire it, but wasn't quick enough.

* Ruiz was a medieval poet of Spain. The following lines are in praise of short women.

The little gun bucked as it went off. I heard the bullet hit the desk back of me. There was a sharp burn on my wrist from the gases from the muzzle. I twisted the gun from her hand and stepped back.

"Now," I said, "maybe we can talk about who you are and who sent you and why you want to kill me. I never thought El Nariz would hide behind the skirt of a woman."

She stared at me, her eyes wide with what might have been either anger or fear. Then, suddenly, she whirled and darted through the door. Her high heels clicked down the hall like machine-gun fire.

I hadn't expected her to bolt, and by the time I reached the doorway, she had already almost reached the stairs at the end of the corridor. I still would have taken after her, but already several office doors had popped open. I slipped the little gun in my pocket before anyone could see it.

The lawyer who had the office next to mine looked out and spotted me. "Heard something like a shot," he said.

"Me, too," I said innocently. "I looked out, but all I saw was a girl running. And there don't seem to be any corpses around. Guess it was a false alarm."

"Sounded like a shot," he insisted. "Sounded like it came from your office."

"Oh, that," I said. "Must have been me opening a bottle of soda. Always have a nice soft drink about this time every afternoon."

"Didn't sound like that," he said. He was the stubborn kind. Probably an ambulance chaser, I decided. "Think we ought to call the police?"

"Why not?" I said cheerfully. "They just love to have people call and report noises that sound like shots." I turned and went back into my office, closing the door.

It didn't take long to find the hole in my desk. I used a knife to dig the bullet out. It was a .25. I tossed it into the wastebasket. I took the gun out of my pocket. It was a real cute little gun. And it was pastel blue. I removed the clip and tossed it and the gun in a drawer of the desk. I'd keep it as a souvenir, even though it wouldn't be of any use to me. If I had to use a gun, I wanted to be sure it was going to stop a man quick.

I had just finished when the phone rang. I picked it up and answered. It was Lieutenant Rockland.

"Hi, Johnny," I said. "Got everything all worked out?" I thought I'd beat him to that line.

"Not quite," he said. "But I was right."

"How?"

"The taxicab didn't help us any. At least fifty different prints in it, but the steering wheel had been wiped clean. Also, we found out this morning that Perrola's plane did land at a New Jersey airfield. Was there about thirty minutes and took off again. The man there wasn't sure whether someone else got aboard or not. Perrola claimed he landed to make a phone call."

"Did he?"

"If he did, it was a local call. We checked."

"What about the Miami police?" I asked.

"He never landed there. I checked with someone out at Idlewild this morning, and Perrola has extra tanks on his plane so he doesn't have to stop for gas between New York and

Puerto Torcido. So our friend El Nariz is probably back there safe and sound, and everyone will deny ever hearing of him."

"If he went," I said, "he left a friend behind."

"What do you mean?"

"A broad," I said. "She came in here a few minutes ago and was going to shoot me."

"Who was she?"

"How the hell do I know?" I said. "She was small and pretty and she had a gun."

"What happened?" he asked.

"I said boo and she ran away."

"Yeah?" He didn't sound as if he believed it. "Can you describe her?"

"Sure," I said cheerfully. "I'd say she was thirty-five, twenty-two—"

"Okay," he interrupted. "Save your breath. We're not running a brassiere factory and we need a little more than that to look for someone."

"A fine thing," I said, "when innocent citizens get threatened by guns and the police won't do anything."

He had an answer for that. A short, Hemingway-type word. That seemed a good point at which to end the conversation, so I did. I finished tidying up the office, then I left and went down to the Village. I kept my eyes open, but no one else appeared waving guns. I bought a paper and headed for my favorite restaurant. The hostess was even prettier and she didn't wave a single gun. After dinner I went home and curled up with a good book. Everything was as quiet and peaceful as if I'd never heard of the Monican Republic.

I was up early the following morning and after breakfast started my packing. I had two problems. One was to get a couple of guns into the country with me and the other was to take the fake manuscript in without its being seen. Any way I worked it, there was going to be a gamble. If they made a thorough enough search at Monican customs, they'd find everything, no matter what I did. But from what I knew about the Torcido tactics, I didn't think they'd do that. A lot of Torcido's enemies had gone to the Monican Republic. They'd never had any trouble getting in; getting out was the problem.

After thinking it over, I decided on a suitcase that had a false bottom in it. Nobody would be fooled if they were doing a real search, but it would pass a perfunctory one. I put two guns, both .32s, and the shoulder holster under the false bottom and then packed my clothes. I had a ream of type-writer paper in a box. I took out most of the paper and then put my fake Spanish manuscript in and put some of the paper on top of it. Again, it was something that would pass only if the customs examination was routine. Just to help it along slightly, I tossed in three extra cartons of cigarettes. I knew that regulations permitted me to take only one carton into the country.

Then I got dressed and went down and took a cab to Idlewild. I got there a good half hour before the flight time. I checked my bag in at the Pan American counter and picked my seat on the plane. Then I went into the bar and ordered a martini. I sat, sipping it, and stared idly out at the Pan American counter. Not that I was watching it for any particular reason, but there wasn't anything else to look at and I thought

I might as well see what my fellow passengers looked like. There might even be a pretty girl on the flight.

There was. I watched her check her bags at the counter and it was only when she started to turn away that I realized why she was familiar. The last time I'd seen her, she'd been holding a pastel blue gun pointed right at me.

I watched her go into the drugstore, then I went back out to the counter. I showed the man my ticket and said I'd like to take another look at the seating arrangements. He brought out the chart. Only one additional name had been added to it since I last looked at it. A seat in the tail of the plane. Number 27, next to the window. The name was Sanjurjo.

"I think," I told the man behind the counter, "I would like to change my seat."

"Your name?" he asked. He'd already handed my ticket back to me.

"March."

He looked on the chart. I was down for a window seat up front. He looked up. "Something wrong, Mr. March?" he asked.

"Nothing wrong," I said. "I just heard that we may hit some strong winds between here and Miami. I always prefer to sit in the back when there are strong winds."

He looked at me suspiciously. "There hasn't been any change in the weather forecast."

"Then I must have heard it wrong in the beginning," I said blandly. "Anyway, I promised my wife that I'd always sit in the tail of the plane if it's a rough trip."

He didn't believe me, but there wasn't anything that

warranted him saying so. "Where would you like to sit, sir?" he asked.

"My lucky number is twenty-seven," I said innocently. "How about that?"

"The aisle seat is free," he said. He sounded even more suspicious. He probably still remembered the pretty little brunette who had just been there.

"Fine," I said. "I'll take that. Do you mind fixing it up?" I handed him my ticket again.

He removed the seat stub from my ticket and put a new one on. Then he made the changes on the chart. But he still didn't like it. He decided to try a gambit. "Do you know the young lady, sir?" he asked.

I looked over my shoulder as if I thought he was referring to someone there. "What young lady?" I asked.

"Sorry, sir," he said. "I guess I misunderstood." He handed my ticket back to me.

"Perfectly all right, it's liable to happen to anyone," I said. I grinned at him. "She was pretty, wasn't she?" I walked off before he could answer and went back to my martini in the bar.

I stayed there until the last call for the plane to the Monican Republic. Then I went out and down the ramp. I showed my ticket to the man at the gate and then I made what always seems like the last, long walk from the gate to the plane and up the steps. Condemned men can't really feel worse because they've at least had a last meal. The stewardess looked at my ticket and told me where to go. As if I didn't know.

She was already in the window seat, looking small, dark, beautiful, and remote.

She didn't look around as I sat down next to her. I didn't say anything, but busied myself buckling on my safety belt and making myself comfortable. I tilted my seat back and sat there watching the soft outline of her face. She kept glancing out the window and chewing nervously on her full underlip.

Finally they slammed the door and wheeled away the stairs. One motor coughed into action, then another. When they were all going, the big plane began to taxi slowly out to the main runway. There the motors roared and it quickly picked up speed until there were no longer any bumps and the ground was dropping away below.

"Ya se acabó," I said.

Out of the corner of my eye I saw her look at me, then heard the quick intake of her breath.

"Is it not pleasant, Señorita," I said, "that we meet again so soon after the first time?"

"I do not understand," she said. Her voice was unsteady, but not too much so. "I have not met you before, Señor."

"But you must remember," I said sadly. "There was only the two of us and nothing but a gun between us. *'Muy graciosa es la doncella, cómo es bella y hermosa!'* "*

"I will call the stewardess," she said.

"Permit me," I said. I reached up and flicked the button that would turn on the light in the stewardesses' compartment.

In a moment a stewardess came hurrying back, her eyes searching for the lighted switch. She was beautiful, but she had an air of efficiency that seemed to say you shouldn't try to make anything out of it.

---

* Ruiz: "The maiden is very charming. How lovely and beautiful she is!"

"Yes?" she said, stopping beside us.

"I will have a dry martini," I said. "Señorita Sanjurjo will tell you what she wishes."

"Nothing," she said.

"It is better to tell her now," I said. "The stewardess is really quite busy and we don't want to keep calling her every few minutes."

"Nothing," she repeated tightly.

"I guess a martini is all, then," I told the stewardess.

She went forward and soon came back with it. She gave it to me with a disapproving look and went on to ask the other passengers if they wanted coffee, tea, or milk. The girl beside me was staring out the window with a fixed, tight-lipped expression.

"When you've seen one cloud," I said, "you've seen them all."

She didn't answer.

"Let's talk about something more pleasant," I said. "Why did you try to kill me?"

"Señor," she said tightly, "I do not know you and I do not wish to talk with you. Unless you stop, I shall ask the stewardess to give me another seat."

"You couldn't improve on the present one," I told her. "I noticed when you were running away from my office yesterday."

She said nothing.

"Why did you want to kill me?" I asked again.

No answer.

"Oh, well," I said. *"Ya pasó aquello.* And I suppose you can always try again in Puerto Torcido. It should be easier there."

She still stared fixedly out of the window. I gave up and finished my martini. I tucked the glass into the pocket of the seat in front of me. I leaned back and relaxed.

"This is your captain speaking," a voice said from a loud-speaker. "We are now at twenty-two thousand feet and flying at an air speed of two hundred and sixty miles per hour. The weather ahead is fine and—"

I fell asleep in the middle of the captain's little speech. Three and a half hours later we landed at Miami and trans-ferred to another plane. This time the girl fooled me. She managed to get into a seat next to another woman and gave me a triumphant look as I went by. I found a seat not very far away and went asleep again almost as soon as we were in the air. As I'd told her, when you've seen one cloud, you've seen them all.

Just nine hours from the time we left New York, the plane came down in Puerto Torcido. We all filed out and into a waiting room in the customs building. There was a short wait while our luggage was unloaded. The pretty little brunette sat by herself over at one end of the room. I lit a cigarette and wandered over.

"Look, honey," I said, "we might as well be friendly about this. Why don't you have dinner with me tonight?" She glanced at me, then looked quickly away.

"We'll make rules about it," I said. "No fair killing me during the soup course, but you can try anytime after the main course. I never liked Spanish desserts anyway. Where shall I call for you?"

"Do me only one favor, Señor March," she said, her voice low. "Leave me alone."

I grinned down at her. "I'm only trying to prove that North Americans are as gallant as our Southern neighbors. The least I can do is give you another chance."

"Please," she said.

"Okay, honey," I said. "But I'll be at the Hotel Torcido. You phone me and we'll make a date." I turned and walked away.

They were soon bringing the bags in and then it wasn't long before I was called up before a small, fierce-looking customs inspector. I unlocked my suitcase and threw the lid open.

"Tiene usted algo que declarar?" he asked.

"Not much," I said lightly. "Let's see, there are two guns, one holster, an ancient Spanish manuscript, the crown jewels of England, and only a small amount of narcotics."

"No es cosa de risa," he said sternly.

I agreed that it was no laughing matter and he looked through my suitcase with a gentle hand and a bored gaze. He lifted the clothes and patted them and that was all. He took the top off the paper box and riffled the top ten or twelve pages. To do all of this, he had pushed aside the cartons of cigarettes as though they didn't exist; then he suddenly seemed to see them for the first time.

"Caray!" he said. "What is this? It is forbidden, Señor, to bring so many cigarettes into the country. You will have to pay duty on these." He separated two cartons from the other one with a finger and looked at me accusingly.

I looked properly contrite and agreed to pay. The matter was soon settled and he closed my suitcase with an air of virtue. I fastened it and left. But by that time the girl was gone. I'd had some idea of trying to follow her, but there was nothing to follow. So I got in a cab and told the driver to take me to the Hotel Torcido.

It was a short ride. The hotel was beautiful and modern, looking as if it might have been transplanted from Miami Beach. I went in and registered. A bellboy took me upstairs. He was probably no more than seventeen, but he had the sort of young-old face you find so often on boys in the Spanish-speaking countries.

"What is your name?" I asked him when we were in the room.

"Hernando," he said.

"I haven't changed any of my money yet," I said. "Is it all right if I tip you with American money?" That was a silly question.

"*Sí, por cierto,*" he said. Then just to make sure that I understood, he added, "Yes."

I took out a five-dollar bill and handed it to him. "I don't know how long I'll be here, Hernando," I said, "but I'm always going to ask for you when I want anything. And there will be others like this if you do a good job."

"*Le estoy muy agredecido,*" he said. "The Señor has but to ask and I will come running."

"You don't have to run, just walk fast," I said. "In about a half hour bring me some ice and a bottle of Canadian Club. Okay?"

"*Está bien,*" he said, and left.

I checked the time. I still had time to make my first move. I picked up the phone and told the operator to get me the presidential palace. When the second operator answered, I said that I wanted to speak to Generalissimo Torcido. She seemed a little startled, but told me to wait a minute. After a while a male voice answered.

"What is it you wish?" he asked me in Spanish.

"My name is Milo March," I told him in the same language. "I am an American just arrived in Puerto Torcido. I would like to see the Generalissimo."

"Why?"

"I am here on a mission for a very wealthy American," I said. "I would like to have the Generalissimo's permission as well as his advice, which I'm sure will be invaluable."

"Aguarda un momento," he said.

I waited the minute and then a couple more. Finally he came back on the phone.

"Señor March?" he said.

"Yes?" I said.

"Generalissimo Francisco Pérez de Calavera Torcido Badajoz will receive you tomorrow morning at ten."

"Thank you," I said and hung up.

I gave the hotel room a quick casing before I did anything else. I had heard that all the hotel rooms in Puerto Torcido were bugged. My search didn't turn up anything, but that didn't mean it wasn't true. In a country where one man owned everything, the bugs might even be built into the rooms. I'd just remember to be careful.

I unpacked. I'd also brought with me a good big roll of adhesive tape. I was quite sure that the Torcido forces knew I was coming, when I got there and why; my pretense of working for Merry Mellany wasn't going to be any more than a disturbing tactic. And I was equally sure that before too long I would have some sort of official visit and that it might be one much more thorough than the customs inspection. I used the adhesive tape to fasten one gun and the holster underneath the springs of the bed. I taped the other gun inside the top of the toilet bowl just above the water line. Then I took a drawer out of the dresser and taped the fake Spanish manuscript under the top of the dresser. I put the drawer back in and filled it with my shirts.

I had barely finished when there was a knock on the door. It was Hernando with the ice and the bottle of Canadian Club. When he left, I made myself a drink and sat down to enjoy it. I wouldn't try to do anything until after I'd made my official visit the following morning. Even then my best bet might be to wait until the Monican underground got in touch with me. They could at least give me some clue as to where to start.

I was working on my second drink when there was another knock on the door.

"Come in," I called, thinking that Hernando was being overly eager.

The door swung open and there were two strange men there. The one in front was of medium size, his thin, dark face dominated by a Roman nose of heroic proportions. There was something about the way he looked at me that stamped him as some sort of official. The second man was clearly an underling.

"Señor Milo March?" the first man asked.

"Yes," I said. But I didn't leave it at that, because I don't like officials to get the first edge. "But there must be some mistake. I've already had room service."

His face tightened a little but that was all. "I am Jorge Carnicero," he said. "The Chief of Police of Puerto Torcido."

"That's nice," I said, "but I didn't call for the police either. I haven't lost anything—so far."

"We have no crime in Puerto Torcido," he said stiffly. There was something familiar about his voice, but I couldn't place it.

"No?" I said. "Then to what do I owe the honor of this visit?"

"We have received confidential information," he said, "that you are friendly with certain enemies of the Monican Republic. Such people are not welcome here, Señor March."

Then I suddenly knew why his voice was familiar. It was the same voice I'd heard on the telephone and then later from a shadowy figure in the night. This was the man who had called himself El Nariz on the phone—the man that Lieutenant Rockland knew as the Monican assassin—and he was the Chief of Police of Puerto Torcido.

FIVE

There was no doubt in my mind. The Chief of Police and El Nariz were one and the same. That also explained why the New York police never got anywhere with their requests for information from the Puerto Torcido Police Department. It certainly added a few complications to my job in the Monican Republic; if nothing else, it was going to make staying alive a little more difficult.

"You say nothing, Señor," he said. "Does this mean you do not deny being an enemy of my country?"

"*Ca!*" I exclaimed. "*Por supuesto que no!* I wasn't even listening to you. I was thinking how familiar your voice is. It sounds exactly like that of a friend of mine—in a manner of speaking."

"So?"

"A friend of mine known as El Nariz," I said.

He glared at me. "Now you dare to make fun of my features?" he said, one hand going to his nose.

"Not at all," I told him. "You possess a magnificent nose. It is a veritable grandfather of a nose. I was referring to your voice, which is just like that of a man who, by coincidence, is known as El Nariz. I don't suppose the name is familiar to you?"

"I do not recall it," he said. He grinned at me. This was the sort of game he liked. He probably liked it even better now since we were playing it on his home field. "Señor March, why have you come to the Monican Republic?"

"I'm glad you asked me," I told him. I pointedly fixed myself a drink without offering him one. "In the United States I am a sort of detective. I have been hired by a wealthy American to come down here and be a history detective."

"What?" he asked.

It was my turn to grin at him. "A history detective. I have to find something of historical note which it is believed is in your country. I am sorry that I cannot be more explicit with you, but in the morning I am seeing Generalissimo Torcido to arrange the necessary permits."

"I think you lie," he said darkly. "You are another interfering American who is trying to say that we had something to do with the disappearance of Moreno."

"Moreno?" I said blankly. "There was a Paddy Moreno who was a welterweight, but you couldn't possibly have known him."

"You play games with me, Señor," he said softly. "It is not wise. I know why you are here. I know that you have been paid by the big insurance company."

"You must have been talking to my friend, El Nariz," I said. "That was his favorite illusion, too."

He said the Spanish equivalent of "bah." He gestured for his companion to come in. "Search the place," he ordered.

It made quite a tableau. I sat quietly, drinking my Canadian Club on the rocks; the Chief stood by the door glaring; and the little detective scurried around making his search. But he didn't find anything.

I've never been much of a flag-waver, but you do have to admit that American cops are more thorough than those in most countries. I would never have gotten away with the hiding places in that room with most American cops, but the little Monican cop missed them. He felt under the mattress but not under the springs. Finally he finished, looked at his chief, and shrugged.

"It is well," the Chief said sternly, but he sounded as if it would have been more well if they'd found something incriminating. "I know that you are lying about your reason for being here, Señor March, and you may be sure that I will keep an eye on you."

"Fine," I said, "only do it somewhere else. I paid for this room as a single and that's the way I want it. Close the door gently behind you as you go out." I waited until he got to the door. "What did you say your name was?"

"Jorge Carnicero," he said.

"The next time, Señor Carnicero," I said, "you'd better shoot straighter than you did the last time—for I intend to."

"We shall see, Señor," he said with a tight smile. He went out and closed the door. I went back to my drink.

The fact that El Nariz was also the Chief of Police made my assignment a little more dangerous, but not very much so. I had known that El Nariz would be gunning for me anyway and that here he would certainly have all the protection he wanted. Maybe it would even be easier this way. For one thing, he might go carefully until he found out what would happen after I saw the Generalissimo. For another thing, maybe he'd be overly confident because it was his home territory. He'd think he could knock me off whenever he wanted to, and I could take advantage of that.

At the same time, I couldn't gamble completely on believing that he would wait to kill me. I got up and took the gun and the holster from beneath the bed. I wouldn't try to take it with me to the Palace the next day, but from now on that gun wasn't going to be far from me.

I poured myself another drink and prowled around the room while I sipped it. I remembered again that the room might be bugged. I didn't find any evidence of it in my room, but that didn't mean it wasn't there. And it fit the kind of thing they'd do. I didn't want to take any chances—not with someone from the underground coming to see me. I called downstairs and had Hernando bring me up a radio. He arrived with it in a few minutes. I plugged it in and found a station with music. I left it on soft, but it could always be turned up if someone arrived and I wanted to talk.

I had almost finished my drink when there was a knock on the door. I looked at my watch. It was almost the dinner hour. I'd already had my visit from the police and I wasn't expecting anyone else—except the guy from the underground. I turned up the radio and went and opened the door.

She was a short one. No more than five-three. With ashen blond hair and the dark skin you find on Spanish blondes. The rest of her was just as nice. She must have been aware that I was looking her over, because when my eyes finally came back to her face, she was waiting, a little smile pulling at the corners of her mouth.

"If this is any kind of mistake," I said in Spanish, "just don't let me find out about it until later. Much later."

"Señor March?" she asked.

"No mistake there," I said. "I'm March."

"I am Señorita Fulano," she said. *"Dichosos los ojos que ven a usted."*

That was the name and the password for the underground. "No," I corrected her. "Happy are the eyes that see *you*. I must admit that I was expecting something different. A man, that is."

She smiled. "There was a man who was supposed to come to see you, but unfortunately he is in prison."

"I am sorry he is in prison," I said, "but not as sorry as I might have been under different circumstances." I had a sudden idea that I liked. "I'm not sure that my room is a good place to talk. I was about to have dinner downstairs. Why don't you join me and we can talk and get acquainted at the same time?"

"Out in the public is a better place to talk?" she asked with a smile.

"Si, por cierto," I said. "In the middle of any sort of crowd is always the best place to tell secrets. No one will then pay any attention—although I can't imagine you not being noticed anywhere. Will you join me?"

"All right," she said.

"Espere un momento," I told her. I went back into the room and put on my jacket. I left the radio on; I might as well entertain the police if they did have a bug on the room. "Okay, let's go," I said.

We went down in the elevator. When we reached the lobby,

the dining room was to the left, but I turned to the right. "I want to test something," I told her. We walked across the lobby straight toward the doors. Just as we reached them, I stopped and looked back. One man had risen from a chair in the lobby and was starting to saunter toward us. He looked like a cop, too. They usually do, no matter what country you're in. I don't care how much people try to tell you differently; put the average cop into a plain business suit and he looks like he's wearing a disguise.

"Now let's go back," I said to the girl. We turned and marched back the way we'd come. The cop slowed up and looked confused. So then I knew I was right. When we reached him, I stopped.

"Tiene usted fósforos?" I asked him.

He looked even more confused, but fumbled around until he found some matches. He handed them to me. I found a cigarette and lit it. Then I handed the matches back to him.

"Le estoy muy agradecido," I said.

"De nada," he muttered.

"In the meantime," I continued, "since I have made the acquaintance of a beautiful young lady, you might say that I am not working tonight. We are merely going into the dining room, so you can again relax in the comfortable chair and dream that you might be as fortunate as I am. Later, when you've finished, you may give my regards to El Nariz."

His face was red with angry frustration as the girl and I went on to the dining room.

"What was that about El Nariz?" she asked as we sat down.

"The Chief of Police," I said. "He has a big nose, so it is what I've decided to call him." I wasn't even going to tell the underground about him; El Nariz was going to be my own personal property.

The waiter came and I ordered a couple of cocktails. We waited until he returned with them. The dining room was about two-thirds full, and the hum of conversation would easily drown out our words for anyone trying to listen from a nearby table.

"Okay," I said to the girl. "You know why I'm here?"

"To find Dr. Moreno."

There was no point in getting technical, so I nodded. "Can you or your friends give me any information?"

"I do not think so," she said. "We have not heard of anyone seeing him here in the Monican Republic. And if he had been here, surely the underground would have heard about it."

"Maybe, maybe not," I said. "For one thing, from what I've heard, there isn't much of an underground."

"That's true," she admitted.

"And he could have been slipped in without any of you knowing it. And what about the American pilot who is supposed to have flown him down here and then was killed?"

"He was working for the Monican Airlines," she said. "He had an argument with another pilot, Alberto de la Garra, who killed him. The man who killed him was arrested and confessed. The argument was over some private matter."

"And then what happened to de la Garra?"

"He committed suicide in prison. He was very loyal to Torcido and it is said that he realized he'd done something that would cause the government trouble and that this was why he killed himself."

"It's too damned convenient," I said. "All right. So Mike Dayton worked for the Monican Airlines. And de la Garra worked for them. The two guys had an argument and one of them got killed. But why just now? Why not two months ago or two months from now? Why did it happen just before Dayton might be questioned about the mysterious passenger he brought here from New York? And then de la Garra confesses and obligingly cuts his throat. Oh, sure, things like that happen, but it's very seldom that murder and suicide even seem to be convenient for anyone. Life doesn't very often work out so beautifully—without a slight assist from someone."

"Perhaps you are right," she said.

"You can almost bet on it, honey," I said. "I'm going to bet on it until something better comes along." I signaled to the waiter to bring us two more cocktails.

"Now," I said, after he had served them, "it is obvious that you and your people can't give me any information about Moreno at the moment. You may perhaps dig up something while I'm here, and I presume that you will give it to me if you do. Maybe I won't need any other help. But if I do, what can I expect?"

"Anything we can do," she said slowly. "We are not a large group and we do not have much influence here. But perhaps there will be ways we can help. For reasons of safety, and not because we do not trust you, it is better if you do not know many of us. So it has been agreed that I will work with you as much as is possible. That is, I will tell you where I can be reached and I will carry information between you and our group. If you need other help, you may phone me and I will meet you. If it's something I can do, I will; if not, I will take the request to our group."

"Part of the arrangement sounds like one I'd like," I said with a grin. "Tell me, do you have a name or must I continue to call you Señorita Fulano?"

"I am Juana Ramos, Señor March."

"A pretty name," I said. "Despite Spanish tradition about formality, it does not go well with underground movements. I'll call you Juana, and suppose you try calling me Milo."

"All right, Milo," she said with an answering smile.

"The next step is to order dinner. The underground must be fed." I beckoned the waiter and we ordered. "One more question, Juana. Where was de la Garra in prison when he committed suicide?"

"Here in Puerto Torcido. It is a very old prison called the Fortress of Santa Monica."

"Nice there's something in the place that isn't named after Torcido," I said.

"What are your plans, Milo?" she asked.

I shrugged. "Tomorrow I go to the Palace and meet the Generalissimo. The only other plans I have are to pay much attention to a very lovely woman whom I've just met. I think it might be more fun than looking for Dr. Moreno."

The waiter started bringing the dinner and as we ate we talked of other things. I learned that she was a dancer and that someday she would like to go to the United States and dance. She had once been married but was no longer. She had her own apartment, her parents being dead, and when she wasn't dancing she liked to read. Things like that.

After dinner we went back upstairs. The detective was still sitting in the lobby. We turned the radio up, had Canadian Club on the rocks, and talked some more. At least, for a while. I was right about one thing. It was more fun than looking for Dr. Moreno.

I was up early the next morning and had breakfast in the room. Then I showered and got dressed. I tucked my gun and holster in under my shirts in the dresser and took off for the Palace. A taxi got me there in ten minutes.

I went through a whole battalion of majordomos, clerks, and secretaries. Each one would make a phone call and then pass me on to the next. But I finally arrived with one who seemed a combination of an advertising account executive and a thug. He merely wanted to make sure that I was Milo March and then he led me into a room that was apparently an office although it was large enough to have served as a ball-room. There was a man seated at a rather large, ornate desk at the far end of the room.

"Generalissimo," my companion said, "the American with whom you have the appointment, Señor Milo March."

With that, he withdrew, leaving me standing in the middle of the Turkish-carpeted desert. The man behind the desk stood up, and I gathered that I was meant to approach. I started the long hike, using the distance to take my first look at Torcido.

He was an old man, somewhere in his late sixties, but still straight and firm. He wore a military uniform, patterned after those of American staff officers, but with no insignia. His face was like old rock that had been chipped and gouged at without really being harmed. The hair above it was mostly white. As I drew nearer I saw that his eyes were as much like granite as the rest of his face. His expression might have been called kindly, yet looking at his face it was even easier to believe all the stories that had been told about him.

"Señor March," he said, "it is good of you to visit my country." He held out his hand and smiled. The smile did nothing for his face except to widen his mouth.

"Thank you, Generalissimo," I said. I shook hands with him. His was a strong, unrelenting hand. "I want to also thank you for seeing me. I had doubted it would be possible for a mere American visitor to see one as busy as yourself."

"I always have time for America and Americans," he said. "I have long had an admiration for your country. In my youth, I served in the American army for a time. All of my sons have gone to military schools in America. I am proud of whatever connection I have had with your country. If you have a minute to spare, Señor March, I should like to show you something."

He stepped out from behind the desk and walked swiftly across the room without waiting to see if I had a minute to spare. I followed him. He threw open the doors into another room.

"This," he said over his shoulder, "is my own personal museum. Everything in here has been important to me or is dear to me in some way."

As I followed him into the room, I could see that the walls on either side were lined with glass cabinets. In each one there were objects hanging on the wall or placed on shelves.

"But these," he said, stopping in front of one of the cabinets, "are my proudest possessions."

I gazed through the glass. There was a uniform hanging on the wall. It was an American uniform of the type worn in the First World War. It looked as if it were about to fall to pieces. On a shelf in front of it there was a medal with faded ribbon.

"That is the uniform I wore in the United States Army," the old man said, "and that is the medal I was awarded. Since then I have been decorated with medals from all over the world, but that is the one I am proud of." I looked at it again. As near as I could see it was merely a Good Conduct Medal. But who was I to sneer at that? I'd spent a lot of time in the Army and they'd never given me anything for good conduct.

"I don't blame you, sir," I said.

As I turned away from the cabinet, I caught sight of a large table a few feet away. There were several guns and knives on it, each one tagged with a white card. There were also several books, a pile of newspapers, what appeared to be several letters, and two manuscripts. One of them had a blue cover.

"I see that you are looking at the table," Torcido said evenly. "It contains many souvenirs of attempts to destroy me."

Until that moment I hadn't been sure whether Torcido would know why I was there or not. It was highly possible that he would not be informed of everyone who was looking for information against him. But then I knew he had been told, from the way he was watching me, with those eyes like old stone, the way an animal watches its prey. And I knew why. I happen to be quite farsighted and even at that distance I could read the lettering on the front of the manuscript with the blue cover. It was *The Bloody Reign of Torcido* by Jaime Moreno.

"Would you like to look at them?" he asked softly.

"Not especially," I said casually. "At least, not at the moment." I turned and looked into another cabinet where there were a number of ornate silver cups. Two of them, I noticed, were for horsemanship. "Someday before I leave the Monican Republic I would like very much to come back and see the entire museum, if you will grant me that privilege. I would prefer, however, to do it after I have concluded my business in the Monican Republic, when I can perhaps devote myself to some moments of leisure."

"It will be my pleasure," he said. "You may call at any time and make an appointment. I myself will personally conduct you through this room. And you must forgive me, Señor March, for stealing this much time from your business. I'm an old man and sometimes I forget that there are young men who are in a hurry." He didn't mean any of it, especially the part about being an old man. You could tell by the way he looked and moved that he thought he could still take anyone regardless of age. And maybe he could.

He turned and led the way back into the office and seated himself behind his desk. "And now what can we do for you?" he asked briskly. "You will find that the facilities of my country are always at the disposal of North America and North Americans."

"I want permission," I said carefully, "to search throughout your country for a certain manuscript, and if I'm successful, permission to take it back to the United States."

I almost got him with that. Something finally stirred in those dark eyes for a second, then he got it under control. "A manuscript?" he said. "I do not understand."

"I will explain," I said. "Normally, back in the United States, I am what you might call a sort of detective. I work for insurance companies trying to solve crimes that are committed against them. My present mission here, however, has nothing to do with that. I am working for an individual."

"You left something out of your background, Señor March," he said. "When I was told yesterday that you had phoned for an appointment, I thought there was something familiar about your name and I asked someone to make a few discreet inquiries. You left out your own service in the Army, where you still hold the rank of Major and for which you were awarded several medals. That was why I thought you might be interested in that one cabinet in my museum."

"I didn't think it important," I said. I wondered why he was mentioning it. Just to show me that they'd checked up on me?

"And you forgot to mention," he went on, "that you have been recalled several times in recent years and assigned to work for the Central Intelligence Agency. You have made quite a reputation as a fighter of world Communism, Major March. That is why I was willing to see you. It is a subject which interests me and one where, if I may say so, I have made some small contributions myself."

"I'm well aware of that," I said. Now it was beginning to make some sense. They knew that I was supposed to be working for the insurance company, but something else was bothering them. That was my CIA background. A man had been kidnapped from American soil and an American had been murdered because of his participation.

They were wondering if I was actually there representing the CIA instead of the insurance company. Well, let them wonder; the more confused they were about what I was doing and why, the better it would be for me. In the meantime I'd stick to my other little story; it was poor, but it was my very own.

"I didn't mention any of those things," I continued, "because they have no bearing on my present mission. I imagine that you've heard of Miss Merry Mellany?"

"The Mellany Oil Company?" he asked.

I nodded. "The same. She's already the world's third or fourth richest woman and getting richer by the minute. Lately she's gotten interested in historical objects of the early Americas. She's started to collect them. I believe the idea is that she intends to establish a Mellany Room or Mellany Gift for some museum. She is the one who hired me to come down here."

"I fail to see," he said, "what that has to do with my poor country or with the manuscript I believe you mentioned." I had him on the ropes a little then. Just a little. But enough to make me happy.

"As you know," I said gravely, "historical records show that Christopher Columbus landed on this island. We know that he spent some time in this area before moving on to what is now the Dominican Republic. Miss Mellany has received information which makes her believe that somewhere in your country there is an original manuscript written in the hand of Christopher Columbus. Probably now in the possession of some family who doesn't even know what they have. Miss Mellany has sent me down to try to find it—providing, of course, that we have your permission."

He blinked and you could almost see the wheels turning in his head. "A Columbus manuscript? How would you propose locating it if it does exist?"

"Two methods. One, I will place an ad in local newspapers saying that I'm interested in seeing any old manuscripts that may be in the possession of Monicans. Two, I thought of hiring a car and going around to the really old homes in the country and asking permission to look through any family heirlooms or antiques. We will, of course, pay the family if we find the manuscript. I might also mention that it is Miss Mellany's intention, should we find it, to have it known as the Torcido Manuscript."

Then I held my breath, for I knew the gamble I was taking. He could knock everything into a cocked hat by just refusing permission and I'd be left with my bare face hanging out. But I didn't think he would. If my story was true, he wouldn't want to miss the chance to do a favor for a rich American and at the same time have his name attached to something of historical importance. If it wasn't true, he'd still want me around within reach while he felt the situation out.

I was beginning to feel that my position was better than I had planned. Thanks to their own suspicions, they now had three choices. They knew from El Nariz that I had been hired by the insurance company presumably to locate Moreno. They suspected that I might be using that as a front while actually working for the CIA and looking for Moreno and the murderer of Dayton, the American pilot. Now I'd given them a third possibility. Of course, they'd check on it as quickly as possible. And Merry Mellany would tell whoever checked that it was true.

That would leave them with some uncomfortable alternatives. If they were certain I was only working for the insurance company and I stumbled onto anything, it would be easy to arrange an accident. My position then would hardly be legal and nobody would do much of anything except shout. If I were working for the CIA, it was another matter and one that might be dangerous no matter how handled. If, in addition to trying to find Moreno, I was really working for Merry Mellany, then I had on the surface a legitimate reason for being there, and a very rich American back of me, so that, too, could cause an international problem if anything happened to me. On the other hand, they didn't dare let me find and get away with anything that would tie Torcido to a kidnapping and maybe two or three murders.

All of this, I was sure, was running through Torcido's mind as he stared at me with his expressionless eyes. But I felt certain that, if nothing else, I had bought a few days' time during which El Nariz would be told not to pull any triggers unless he caught me in the act of getting something on them.

"I suppose those methods would work," Torcido said finally. "You say you are authorized to act as Miss Mellany's agent?"

I let my breath out slowly. "Yes."

"Would you be willing to give us a document, signed on

her behalf, stating the use to which the manuscript would be put if found?"

I nodded. "I'll write it out right now if you like."

"No need," he said, waving his hand. "When you return to your hotel you may write it out and send it over. We will then send to you the permissions you require." One of his hands disappeared beneath the desk for a minute.

"Thank you," I said.

"De nada," he said. "Now, as I told you, when you desire to come up and see my little private museum, I shall be most happy to show you through it personally. As for your mission, we shall offer you every cooperation and I only regret that I cannot also do that personally. But the pressures of my office make it necessary to entrust you to one of my men. You may rest assured, however, he will do everything for you that I would."

I heard the door back of me open.

"You wished to see me, Excellency?" a man's voice asked. It was a curiously cultivated voice yet with a silky hardness to it that is seldom associated with such a voice.

"Yes, come in, Raimundo," Torcido said.

I turned to look at the newcomer and recognized him immediately. Like everyone else who reads a newspaper, I had seen his photograph many times. This was Raimundo Perrola, the international playboy, diplomat for the Monican Republic, a man who specialized in marrying rich women, and who was believed by many to be the finger man in all the killings ordered by Torcido. He looked to be about fifty, although his black hair was generously streaked with gray. He was, I suppose, handsome by almost any standards, but there was a kind of aloof cruelty in his face. He was well dressed, looking as if he'd just stepped out of the pages of a men's fashion magazine.

"Raimundo," Torcido said, "this is Señor Milo March from America. Señor March, Señor Raimundo Perrola."

"Señor March," Perrola said. He gave me a manly handshake—almost too manly, as though he were trying to prove something.

"Señor March is here on a mission for a wealthy American lady," Torcido said, "for which we have granted permission. You will give him any assistance he may wish."

"With pleasure," Perrola said.

"I am delighted to have met you, Señor March," Torcido went on. "Please remember to call for an appointment whenever you wish to see my museum. In the meantime, I wish you success with your mission." It was clearly my dismissal.

"Thank you, Generalissimo," I said, and looked at Perrola.

"We will go to my office," he said. He led the way toward the door. We had just reached it when Torcido spoke again.

"Señor March," he said.

I looked around.

"Your army records, I am told," he said, "show you to be a very clever man. I flatter myself that I am a keen observer of men. After spending these few minutes with you, it occurs to me that you may be more clever than the records show. Either that or one of the bravest men I have ever met."

"You flatter me, Your Excellency," I said. "In the army, one is considered clever if he can add two and two. And nothing could require less bravery than my present mission. A manuscript can hardly fight back. And with your kind permission to look for it, who would dare try to stop me?"

"Who would dare indeed?" the old man murmured. It was impossible to tell if he was being ironic. *"Adiós."*

"Adiós," I said, and turned and followed Perrola into the corridor. We went down it for three or four doors and turned in to another office. It was a replica of Torcido's except that it was smaller. Perrola waved me to a chair beside his desk.

"Do you mind if we use English, Mr. March?" he asked. "You speak excellent Spanish, but I must confess I've become more at home in your language or French than in my own."

"Okay," I said. "Of course, I recognize you from your pictures, and I'm rather surprised to find you here. I thought your headquarters was in Paris."

"Officially it is," he said, "but I am actually ambassador-at-large, which means that I go wherever it becomes necessary to solve some little problem. As a matter of fact, I just returned from New York City." It seemed to me that he was watching me as he said it.

"Oh?" I said politely. "A social visit, or was there a little problem to solve?"

"A very small one," he said with a wave of his hand. "It was nothing. But this mission of yours, Mr. March—did I hear you say it involved a manuscript?"

"Yes. My client believes that there is an original Christopher Columbus manuscript somewhere here in the Monican Republic, and I have been commissioned to try to find it."

"The client would be the wealthy American lady, I suppose. Would it be indiscreet to inquire who she is?"

"Miss Merry Mellany."

His eyebrows went up. "Really? I've never had the good fortune to meet her, but I understand that she is most charming."

"She is," I agreed.

"You know her well?" he asked.

"Quite well," I said.

"I've always wanted to meet her," he said. "Oh, well, I confess the ladies are my one weakness, but I presume we must get to business. What can I do to assist you and the charming Miss Mellany?"

"I don't believe anything at the moment," I said. "I intend to place ads in the papers and to hire a car with a driver who knows his way around and visit some of the old homes where there might be antiques. So at the moment, I'm going to go back to the hotel, write a note to the Generalissimo, call my ad in to the papers, and then do something about hiring a car and getting started."

"There, at least," he said, "I can help you. There are many cars to hire in Puerto Torcido but, alas, not all of them are reliable. Nor are all the drivers."

There were three phones on his desk. He pulled one of them to him and dialed a number. I was sure he was going to load the dice a little, but it didn't make much difference. If I was going to be watched, it might just as well be someone with me as a guy trailing a hundred yards behind.

"Perrola here," he said a moment later. "There is a Señor

Milo March from the United States—" He looked up at me and asked, "Where are you staying?"

"Torcido Hotel," I said.

"—staying at the Torcido Hotel," he continued into the phone. "He wishes to rent a car and a driver for several days, but it must be a good car and the driver must know every inch of our country. The Benefactor is most anxious that everything possible be done for Señor March. You will take care of this at once?" He listened and nodded. "Good, good." He hung up and smiled at me. "The best car and driver in the Monican Republic will be at your hotel waiting for you when you need it. What else can I do for you?"

"Nothing at the moment," I said.

"One cannot work all the time," he said. "Perhaps you would like to meet some people. A charming young lady or two?"

"No, thanks," I said dryly. "I already met a charming young lady last night. In fact, she was quite delightful."

"Ah," he said. He kissed the tips of his fingers. "Life would be very dull if it weren't for the ladies, eh? Well, if there's anything I can do for you—anything at all—please call on me. You may even phone this number at night and they will tell you where to find me."

"You are too kind," I said.

"Not at all. His Excellency liked you. I can tell. And when he likes someone, nothing is too good for that person. Besides, it is my pleasure to extend help to a representative of the charming and beautiful Miss Mellany."

"I'm sure she'll be grateful," I said, which was what

he wanted to hear. "Well, thanks for everything. If I need anything I'll let you know."

"Please do that," he said. He gave me another one of those manly handshakes and I went on my way with my fingers tingling.

I left the Palace and took a taxi back to the hotel through the wide, curving streets. It was a beautiful city, with all the bright allure of the Caribbean. It was difficult, seeing it this way, to fully realize all the corruption and oppression that were hidden somewhere beneath the layers of bright sunshine.

When I reached the hotel, I looked up Hernando and told him to bring me some ice. I went on up to my room and he was there almost as soon as I was. I made myself a drink and thought for a minute about the morning. I had undoubtedly bought myself some time, but there was no way of telling how much. The result was to make me feel like a pig being fattened for slaughter. But it might be all right. I'd just have to be careful. There were two things I could make use of. One was their confusion over who I actually worked for, and the other was the fact that Raimundo Perrola was quite obviously hoping that I might prove a one-way street to Merry Mellany and her millions. I could almost hear him panting every time he mentioned her name.

In the meantime I knew that the Moreno manuscript was still in existence. And I knew where it was. All I had to do was find some way to steal it practically out of Generalissimo Torcido's back pocket. As Martin Raymond would have said, a small problem.

I got out a piece of paper and worked out the ad I wanted to run. Then I got on the phone and called the two local newspapers. I dictated the ad to each of them and told them to bill me at the hotel. Then I wrote a note to Torcido. I told him that if I found the Columbus manuscript and if it proved authentic, Miss Merry Mellany would make it part of a Mellany Room in some United States museum and that the manuscript would be known as the Torcido Manuscript. It sounded all right, so I signed it, sealed it, and addressed it to Torcido at the Palace.

The phone rang. It was the desk telling me that my car and driver were waiting. I said I'd be down shortly and hung up. I took off my coat, then got my holster and gun from the dresser drawer. Just because they were maybe going to give me some free time didn't mean I should stop wearing a watch. I buckled on the holster. I checked the gun and slipped it into the holster. Then I put on my coat.

I picked up the phone and gave Juana's number to the operator.

"*Buenos días*, Juana," I said when her sleepy voice answered.

"*Buenos días*, Milo," she said. "Where are you?"

"At the hotel. I just came back from the Palace, where the red carpet was rolled out for me. Now I'm about to go for a ride in the country."

"Oh," she said. "I am sorry, Milo, I cannot go with you. I have to rehearse today for a new show."

"You couldn't go anyway," I told her. "This is business."

"Oh," she said again. She sounded as if she were pouting. "What time—oh! It is a good thing you called when you did. I have to leave in less than a half hour for rehearsal."

"I'll stop by and drive you there," I said. "Get dressed."

"All right," she said. Then her voice softened. "Thank you, Milo."

"For what?"

"For being so nice. Last night and now."

"It's just part of the regular service," I said. "See you in a few minutes."

I hung up and went downstairs. The driver was waiting for me in the lobby. He was a slender but wiry-looking fellow with black flashing eyes and a quick smile. Someone must have been waiting to point me out to him, for he came to meet me almost as soon as I left the elevator. "Señor March?" he said.

I nodded.

"I am Luis Alejandro Federico Leonardo Argensola," he said, "but you may call me Luis. I am at your service, I and my car, which is the best car in all the country. What is your desire?"

"Where is your car?" I asked him.

"This way, Señor" he said. He darted away toward the front doors. I followed. We got out on the sidewalk and there was an almost new Cadillac sedan.

"Is she not beautiful, Señor?" he asked. "Look at her lines, like those of a beautiful woman. See how she shines, like the eyes of a woman in love. Admit it, Señor."

"She is beautiful," I said. "Will she also run?"

"Like a dream, Señor. You will soon see." He opened the door for me and held it while I got in. He closed the door and got in behind the wheel. He started the motor. *"Adónde va usted?"*

I gave him Juana's address and we were off. He drove fast, like most drivers in this part of the world, but skillfully.

"Does she not run beautifully, like the swallow in flight, Señor?" he asked.

"She runs beautifully, Luis," I said. I decided I liked him even if he might be drawing a little extra money for reporting what I did. "Look, Luis, we may spend considerable time together the next few days, so why not start calling me Milo instead of Señor?"

He flashed me a smile. "Very well, Don Milo. I am honored by your request. *Quien á vos, á mí onora; á mí esperne quien á vos.*"* He gestured eloquently with his shoulders. "Who honors you honors me; he despises me who despises you."

"I am touched, Luis," I said dryly. "Incidentally, what is all this service costing me per day?"

"Ten dollars the day. That is for the car, the gasoline, the driving, and the pleasure of my company." He gave me another smile.

"A bargain," I admitted.

"The money is important, Don Milo," he said. "I admit this to you. Without money I would sit in the shade. For money there is almost nothing I would not do. But it is not all money. Some of it is in here." He struck himself on the chest with one hand.

"I appreciate it," I told him gravely.

He swerved the car into the curb and we were there. Juana was already standing in front of her place waiting. She had

---

* These words appear in a verse of Fernán Pérez de Guzmán, a medieval Spanish poet; they may be based on 1 Samuel 2:30 ("Those who honor Me I will honor, and those who despise Me will be lightly esteemed").

not only gotten dressed in that short time but managed to look as if she'd spent hours making herself beautiful. I opened the door and she got in.

"Where are we going?" I asked her.

"Club Aprieto," she said.

"Do you know where it is?" I asked the driver.

"Luis Argensola knows where everything is," he said. The car shot away from the curb and turned right at the next street.

Juana and I talked as we rode. Nothing important. Just casual man and woman talk, getting acquainted again as if the previous night had never existed. Sometimes when intimacy comes too quickly, you have to start all over again.

Luis soon pulled up in front of the club.

"I have to hurry," Juana said, "but I will see you tonight, yes?"

"You will see me tonight, yes," I said. "Call me when you get back to your apartment and then we'll make our plans."

She nodded and I walked her to the club door. When I went back, I got into the front seat with Luis.

"Now, Luis," I said, "for the next few days I want to go to all the really old homes in the Monican Republic. It doesn't make much difference where we start. I leave that up to you."

"Old homes?" he said, wrinkling his face. "Are you one of those professors who write books about old homes?"

"No. I am searching for something very old and perhaps I will find it in such a home. I will ask the owners for permission to see any heirlooms they might have. If I find what I'm looking for, I will offer to buy it from them."

"It will be expensive?" he asked.

"Probably."

"What is it you look for?" he asked casually. "Perhaps I might find it somewhere."

"I will know it when I see it," I said, "and I'm willing to look at all sorts of things. But I don't want something that has just recently been made to look old."

"You think I would do such a thing, Don Milo?" he asked. "You wound me deeply." But he didn't sound wounded.

In the meantime we had left the city and were driving along a broad, sweeping highway on which there was practically no traffic. It was a beautiful road, except for one thing: every mile or so there was a police post, and just before it was reached there would be a sharp dip in the road so that the car would have to slow up to about twenty miles per hour. Nobody was ever going to make a fast getaway in the Monican Republic.

"You are from the United States, Don Milo?" Luis asked.

"Yes."

"You have been here long?"

"Only since yesterday."

"*Caray!*" he said. "You are fast workers, you *norteamericanos*. You arrive yesterday and already you are a good friend with one of the most beautiful women in Puerto Torcido. It is a gift."

"You know her?" I asked.

"I have seen her dance. Like a flame. But I, Luis Argensola, am a judge of beautiful cars and beautiful women. And she is small. Small women are the best and the most beautiful."

"How do you arrive at that?" I asked.

"It was first said by a great poet," he said. " '*Quiero vos*

abreviar la predicación, que siempre me pagué de pequeño
sermón, e du dueña pequeña et de breve razón, ca lo poco e
bien dicho finca en el corazón.' " He smiled. "I should like
to cut my preaching short for you since I have always done
better with short sermons, short ladies, and short arguments.
For that which is small and well put stays in the heart."

" 'Cupid,' " I said gravely, skipping a part of it, " 'asked me
to speak well of the short ones and to speak of their noble
qualities. I should like to tell you them now. I would say of
short ladies that you take them in jest. They are as cold as
snow and they burn like fire.' "

He looked at me startled. "You know the poetry of the great
Juan Ruiz?" he asked.

"Fourteenth-century in Spain," I said. " 'Small women
are cold outside but burning when in love; in bed they are
comfortable, happy, cheerful, and gay; in the house they are
sensible, peaceful, and virtuous. You will learn much more,
so pay attention to it.' "

"Caray!" he said in delight. " 'In a small precious stone
there is great value and in very little sugar there is great sweetness, and in a small woman there is great love. Few words are
enough for a man with a good head. The seeds of the sweet
pepper are small but they are more comforting and warming
than the nutmeg; it is the same with a small woman; If she
gives you complete love, there is no pleasure in the world
that is not to be found with her.' "

I jumped ahead of him to the end. " *'Siempre quis' muger*
chica más que grande nin mayor, non es desaguisado del
grand mal ser foidor; del mal tomar lo menos, dízelo el sabi-

dor: por ende de las mugeres la mejor es la menor,' " I said.
" 'I have always liked a small woman better than the bigger
ones. It is not imprudent to flee a great evil; of evils take the
smaller, says the wise man: therefore, the smallest of women
are the best.' "

"Qué hombre!" Luis exclaimed. He glanced at me. "Imagine
a *norteamericano* knowing such things. In a way, it saddens
me; but in another way it does not, for those who have known
the poetry of Juan Ruiz have lived fully."

While we had been talking, Luis had turned off the main
highway and we were now climbing steeply up into the hills
on a narrow, rough road.

"Why is it any more strange for a North American to know
of Juan Ruiz," I asked, "than for a taxi driver?"

"Don Milo," he said with dignity, "I am descended from the
Spanish poet Lupercio Leonardo de Argensola. Poetry runs
in my veins as does water in the river. I myself would have
been a poet were life not so hard. There is no doubt of it. Here
in the Monican Republic one must work hard just to exist; it
is difficult to sing new songs when one slaves. But someday,
Don Milo, I shall make enough money. Then I will go to your
United States and sit beneath a tree and I will make the songs
such as even my ancestor did not."

"I hope so, Luis," I said. "I'm not sure that's the best place
to write poetry either, but it is certainly better than here.
Where are we going?"

"There is a house on top of the hill," he said. "It is such as
you said you wanted. We will see."

We did, but not for another fifteen minutes. Then we arrived on the very peak of the hill. In every direction one could see for miles, even to the Caribbean, and it was a breathtaking sight. Luis was right; there was a house up there. Old and weather-beaten, its Spanish lines beginning to fade before the elements. It certainly no longer belonged to anyone who was very rich, but neither was it the home of a peasant.

"A family named Rivelles lives there," Luis said as he stopped the car in front of the house. "I do not know them, but I do know that their family has lived here as long as there has been a Monican state. Perhaps they will have what you wish. We shall see."

We got out and went up to the house. I introduced myself and went through my little spiel. The people were very nice. They began to bring out whatever heirlooms they had and I sat and went through the long farce of looking at them and shaking my head. This was going to be the tough part of the process, but I had to go on the assumption that I was going to be watched pretty steadily, if not by Luis, then by some-one else. If I toured these outlying houses for a few days, then maybe I could begin looking in Puerto Torcido, where I would also get a chance to ask some questions about other things.

By the time I finished looking at everything they had, Luis was about to go to sleep. A few days of this and he wouldn't pay so much attention to what I did. I thanked the family for all their trouble, slipped some coins to two small children, and Luis and I went back to the car.

"Where to now?" I asked cheerfully.

"We will go down the road on the other side," he said,

pointing. "Almost at the bottom of the hill there is another old house."

He started the car and we headed downhill. It was just as steep as coming up and was worse. The road wound aimlessly around and was barely wide enough for the car. On the left side there were sandbanks and sometimes stretches of almost flat grass; on the right side there was an almost straight drop from the very edge of the road.

I suddenly became aware that we were going pretty fast. I glanced at the speedometer. The needle was already past fifty and still moving. At that rate if we met anyone coming up the hill someone was going to be out of luck.

"Luis," I said, "don't you think you'd better slow up just a little? We're not out to win a cup."

"It is not too fast," he said. "Is it not a beautiful car?"

"It is, but will it be if you keep this up? I think the beautiful paint might get scratched if we went over the side of the road."

"I, Luis Argensola, am the best driver in the Monican Republic," he answered.

"Then I'm glad I don't have one of the others," I admitted. I looked at the speedometer again. Now it was past sixty. "Luis," I said firmly, "I hate to disillusion you about the courage of North Americans, but this is too fast."

"Not dangerous," he grunted.

"Okay, it's not dangerous. But I don't like it. So do something about it."

He shrugged. "Well, if you insist ..."

"I do," I said firmly.

He straightened in his seat and put his foot on the brake pedal. Nothing happened. We just kept careening down that crazy road, picking up speed.

"Dios mío," Luis said. He lifted his foot and jabbed again. Still nothing happened.

"The brakes are no more," Luis said, his voice going higher. "I cannot stop it, Don Milo. There is nothing to do but jump. Open your door and jump. *Dios mediante!"* He took one hand from the steering wheel and reached for his door.

SIX

When Luis told me to jump, without thinking I looked out the window on my side. There just wasn't anywhere to jump except straight down. The road ended two feet from the car's wheels and there was a drop of a thousand feet or more. I looked back at Luis. He still had one hand on the wheel and had his door partly open. He was looking ahead for a place to jump.

Then a funny thing happened. I suddenly remembered something Luis had said when we were coming up the other side of the mountain. He'd said that it made him a little sad that I knew the poetry of Juan Ruiz, but then he'd added that it didn't make him too sad because anyone who knew Ruiz had lived fully. Or something like that. And remembering it gave me an idea.

I pulled the gun from my holster and leaned over and pressed the muzzle against his neck.

"If you try to jump, Luis," I said, "I'll pull the trigger."

"For the love of God, Don Milo," he said. "Any minute the car will go over the side of the mountain."

"Then we go together," I said. "Two lovers of Juan Ruiz. Unless you use the brakes—carefully but quickly."

"The brakes are gone," he almost screamed.

"Are they?" I asked gently.

Slowly, as though there were a great weight attached to it, he brought his left hand away from the door handle and put it back on the steering wheel. His foot went carefully down on the brake pedal and I could feel the brakes take hold gently. The car was doing almost seventy by this time, so that even the braking was a delicate task. Too much brakes and we'd skid off the road. But Luis was a good driver. He kept applying pressure lightly and the speedometer needle began dropping back.

I took the gun away from his neck, but held it pointed in his direction. I took my first deep breath in several minutes. It seemed as if hours had passed, but I knew it had probably been no more than three or four minutes. The speedometer dropped to sixty, then to fifty, forty—and finally thirty. Luis's face was dripping with sweat and a muscle was twitching near the corner of his mouth.

"Don Milo, I swear—" he began.

"Don't," I said. "You see how one thing leads to another? You start out by only wanting to commit murder and you end up by wanting to lie. Stop now or you will overload the ears of the priest in the confessional."

He opened his mouth as if to say something else, then closed it.

"Close the door," I told him, "and keep on driving. You are a good driver."

He slammed the door and drove on down the hill at a slow pace. Finally we reached the bottom and the road widened. A hundred yards ahead it joined the main highway.

"Not even an old mansion as you promised," I said. "Oh, well … Pull over to the side of the road and stop."

He did as I told him.

"Shut off the motor," I said.

He turned the key and silence fell around us. There was nothing to be heard but the sound of our own breathing in the car. Now that it was over I could feel myself wanting to shake, but I managed to control it enough to hold the gun steady. Luis glanced at the gun once and then stared straight ahead, both hands still on the steering wheel. There were heavy drops of sweat on his face, but he made no attempt to wipe them away.

I took a package of cigarettes from my shirt pocket with my left hand. I shook one loose and put it in my mouth. I shook another cigarette half out of the package and held it in front of Luis. He hesitated a moment, then took it. I put the cigarettes on the seat between us and got out a book of matches. Using only my left hand, I bent one match out and tucked the flap in under it. I bent it down with my thumb until the head was against the striking surface. A quick flick of my thumb and it flamed. I lit my own cigarette and then held it for him. The feel of the smoke in my lungs was strong but good.

"Who do you work for, Luis?" I asked.

"Myself," he said, looking straight ahead. "Don Milo, I swear before—"

"Before whom?" I interrupted. "Is there a special saint for liars where the penalty is less or you get a wholesale rate?"

He said nothing.

"It is a beautiful car," I said. "It even has beautiful brakes. If I were a poet, I think I'd even write a sonnet to brakes. Who do you work for, Luis?"

He still said nothing.

"I can do one of two things," I said. "I could shoot you carefully through one elbow. If you still didn't talk, I could shoot the other elbow. And after that, through one kneecap, then the other. Few men can go that far without suddenly wanting to talk."

His face had turned paler.

"But," I continued, "I think there might be an even simpler method. I merely make you drive me back to Puerto Torcido and report to Carnicero, the Chief of Police, that you had tried to kill me and failed. ... What is the price of failure in the Monican Republic, Luis?"

The twitch in his face had gotten worse. "I work for Carnicero," he said. "It is true that I have my own taxi business, but I also work for him. He would not like it if he knew that I failed at anything."

"Narrow-minded of him," I said. "He's had a failure or two himself. The pity of it is that you couldn't have really won in this case, Luis. In a way you're lucky you failed, but I doubt if they would appreciate knowing that you're capable of failing. However, it would have been worse for you if you had succeeded."

"I do not understand," he said.

"Of course you don't. Tell me, it was Carnicero himself who told you to come and drive me?"

He nodded.

"After he had orders from the Palace?"

"I do not know from where he had orders. He merely said that you wanted a driver with a car and that you were to be taken care of as soon as possible."

I was remembering back. It must have been Carnicero that Perrola had called. The latter had probably been careful since he was talking in front of me, and that very carefulness had given the police chief the wrong idea. At least, I was pretty sure that Perrola had not been telling him to kill me. There would have been no reason for him to do that. Carnicero already had that in mind; he wouldn't have needed special orders.

"I think," I told him, "that you will find you were given the wrong orders. They want to save me until I'm a bit riper. ... Well, start the car, Luis. We will drive along until we reach a spot where you can make a phone call. You will think of some reason to phone Carnicero, and I think you will find that he'll tell you there's been a mistake. But I shall be standing beside you when you phone, so don't try anything fancy."

"Don Milo, I swear—" he began earnestly.

"Don't bother," I said. "I'm quite sure if there were something in it for you, you'd swear to anything and take your chances in the confessional. Let's go."

He started the car and drove down to the highway. He turned left and the car picked up speed. Within a few minutes we were approaching a dip in the road and a police post. As we neared it, a policeman came out of the tiny building and began waving for us to stop.

"Just in case you want to take a chance with telling them everything," I said, "just remember I can shoot a policeman, too. Once it's gone that far, I'll have nothing to lose." I slipped my gun back into the holster.

"I will say nothing, Don Milo."

"We'll see," I said.

The car rolled to a stop and the policeman came over. He peered through the window at Luis. *"Cómo se llama usted?"* he asked.

"Luis Argensola."

"You are the one," the policeman said. "You are wanted urgently on the telephone. Come."

Luis glanced at me. There was nothing I could do but nod. He got out of the car and followed the policeman. I sat and waited. There was a risk, but I didn't think Luis would say anything. I had an idea that Carnicero was not an easy man to work for; he probably had no tolerance for failure even when it saved him trouble.

Luis was gone about five minutes. Then he came back alone. He slipped behind the wheel and started the car.

He did not say anything until we were well past the police post.

"You were right, Don Milo," he said. "Carnicero had called all the police posts to stop me because he wanted to tell me there should be no accident as yet. I ... ," he broke off.

"You are only to watch and listen to what I do and report it to him each day," I finished for him.

He nodded unhappily. It was beginning to dawn on Luis that he might have been better off if I had shot him back on the mountain. He was hardly in a position to refuse to tell me anything I asked, but if Carnicero ever found out what he was doing, he'd be in even worse shape.

"Tell me, Luis," I said, "why do you work for Carnicero? Are you so fond of Torcido and the government?"

"I spit on them," he said. "On Torcido and his perfumed Perrola and his bloody Carnicero. They are all dung heaps."

"Then why?"

"Money," he said simply. "Don Dinero. And one day I shall go to the United States and lie beneath a tree."

"And write poetry about the men you have killed and betrayed back home?" I asked.

He gave me a hurt look. "Don Milo," he said, "you do not understand. I would not have killed you. There would only have been a little accident."

"Sure," I said. "After which I would have been a little dead."

He shrugged. "If one has led the good life, the saints will protect one from such things."

I glanced at him and he was perfectly serious. "Well," I said, "at least you have the most original rationalization I've ever heard. How much do they pay you for your little services? In dollars."

"Fifty dollars every month," he said proudly. "That is in addition to what I earn driving. I am saving all of it for the day when I can go to the United States."

"I suppose thrift also covers a multitude of sins," I said dryly. "Does that price include special services like the little accident you were going to arrange today?"

"Oh, no. For that I was to receive a bonus of two hundred dollars."

"I don't get it, Luis. You would also have lost your car, and two hundred dollars won't buy another Cadillac."

"Oh, they would also have replaced the car."

I looked at him questioningly.

"The truth, Don Milo," he said, shrugging, "is that this is not my car. My car is a much older one, but when they wish to send me as a driver to wealthy foreigners, they permit me to use this one. It is a beautiful car, is it not? Perhaps one day I can own one like it myself."

"Not on fifty dollars a month," I told him. "I must admit that I hadn't realized corruption came so cheaply down here."

He looked at me reproachfully.

"Sorry, Luis," I said dryly. "I keep forgetting how sensitive you are. I mean I didn't realize that special services were so cheap."

"Everything is cheap but the living," he said.

"Especially the dying."

"Especially the dying," he agreed. "That is the cheapest of all in this country."

"Luis," I said, "how would you like to work for me?"

He glanced at me. "I would like the money," he said honestly. "But working for you while working for Carnicero, would be dangerous, Don Milo. To quit him to work for you would be even more dangerous. It was also Juan Ruiz who said: '*Grande placer et chico duelo es de todo ome querido.*' "

" 'Much pleasure and little grief is every man's desire,' " I repeated. "That is true. And if you work for me also, you will then get the pleasure you work toward much sooner. Carnicero pays you fifty dollars a month. I will pay you that much every two days. Twenty-five dollars a day."

"*Dios mío,*" he exclaimed. "You must be rich. Or the sun has beaten too strongly on your head. How would you pay me this great amount?"

"At the end of each day," I said, "I will give you twenty-five dollars. That is, in addition to what I pay for hiring you and your car."

"*Caray!*" he said. "I, too, must be a fool for listening to you. What would I have to do for this money?"

"Nothing at the present. You can still report to Carnicero what I do each day. Perhaps someday I will not want you to report every single thing I do, but there will be plenty you can report."

"And later?" he asked softly.

"I don't know. There are probably many ways you can help me. But you will not have to arrange any little accidents. If they become necessary, I'll arrange them myself. Then I'll know they don't fail."

"Then it is true that you are not really looking for the old things?"

"True," I admitted. "But every day we'll go looking for some. It'll give you something to report. And that's all you'll report. You'll forget even such things as the fact that I have a gun."

He glanced at me. "You act as if I had already agreed to work for you, Don Milo."

"Twenty-five dollars a day," I said gently.

He sighed. "I am a fool and the son of a fool—but how does a man refuse so much wealth? I will work for you, Don Milo. And probably lose my head."

"You would now lose it quicker by not working for me: And this way you will also have twenty-five dollars each day.

"With that I can buy a new head," he said.

"Besides," I said cheerfully, "if you've lived the good life, the saints will take care of you."

"You use the words as a baker uses dough," he said accusingly. "It is unfair to shape a man's words and then sell them back to him. What is it you look for, Don Milo?"

"Three things. One I've found. Perhaps I'll find the other two. It will be better for you if you do not know more than that. And Luis ..."

"Yes?"

"When a man likes money," I said, "it might occur to him to go to his first employer and say that he has been offered more money by another so that he will gain a promotion. Should such an idea occur to you, flee from it as you would from the devil himself. I think that it might make Carnicero regard you as something less than a brother, and it would not increase your value in my eyes. In fact, I wouldn't be surprised if it became a question of who could get to you first—Carnicero or me."

He shuddered. *"Qué diablos!"* he said. "Why must you talk of such unpleasant matters? It is enough to make one lose faith in his fellow men. You wrong me greatly, Don Milo. I am but a poor taxi driver, but I know better than to tell Carnicero that you even talked to me about anything but old houses. As for you, Don Milo, I shall go every night and light a candle that you remain in good health and stay in our country for many days."

"The twenty-five dollars has nothing to do with it?"

"Ca! Por supuesto que no! Are we not practically blood brothers? Did we not almost die together back there on the mountain?"

"That was a quick rewriting of the script," I said. I laughed. "Luis, you are a rascal. But I have a feeling that we'll get along—while I keep paying you twenty-five dollars a day."

"Que Dios le oiga," he said piously. "Where shall we go now, Don Milo? To look at more old houses?"

"Not if they're on mountaintops," I said. "No, Luis, we've both had a tough day. I think we'll call it quits for today and we'll pick it up again tomorrow. You may take me back to the hotel and then go report."

We drove back into Puerto Torcido and he took me straight to the hotel. I paid him and started to get out.

"I could come around and drive you at night, too," he suggested. "No extra charge," he added.

"I never thought I'd live to see the day," I admitted. "Thanks for the thought, Luis, but I think not. Just that little added touch might make our friends the cops suspicious. Besides, there must be some part of my life that I keep secret from you." He grinned. "Be here early tomorrow. About nine."

"Está bien," he said. He drove off.

I went up to my room and had a good stiff drink of Canadian Club on the rocks. I needed it after that ride down the mountain, even though it was now some time since it had happened. I went into the bathroom and showered and shaved. Then I stretched out on the bed with another drink in my hand and reviewed the day.

It hadn't gone too badly. I knew where Moreno's manuscript was, even if I didn't know how to get my hands on it. I had managed to create enough confusion in Torcido's mind so that for a few days there would be no attempt to kill me.

While I'd had a narrow escape in the process, I was inclined to think that I'd probably hired a valuable assistant. I had no illusions about him. Anything he could turn to his own advantage, he would. But he was smart as well as dishonest, and he was much safer playing along with me than he would be if he tried to double-cross me. The way these Monican boys played, they wouldn't ever again trust anyone who'd even had an offer made to him. And once they didn't trust someone, he probably disappeared shortly afterward. I was sure that Luis knew that. So that plus the twenty-five bucks a day would keep him loyal.

In the meantime, I'd have to give the manuscript hunt a build-up and hope that everybody would get a little bored by the whole thing. Then maybe I could really go to work.

I went out that night with Juana. We had a lot of fun and let it go at that. As soon as I found she had no information for me, I didn't even try to talk about the case. We had dinner out and then went to a club, and I took her home about midnight. There was a detective who followed us almost everywhere except into the bedroom.

Luis was at the hotel early the following morning and we took off for the country again. We visited six old houses and looked at hundreds of antiques. Even I was bored by it.

"But, Don Milo," Luis said, "if you are not looking for the old things, why bother with this? We could drive out into the hills where it is beautiful and just rest until time to return to the hotel. I could still describe what we supposedly had seen. *Caray!* Never in my life did I know so many people kept so many useless things."

"It wouldn't do, Luis," I told him. "Carnicero may not completely trust you; I doubt if he would trust his own mother. So they may have someone else checking up. Besides, these people will also talk about the crazy *norteamericano* who comes and looks at all their old junk and shakes his head and goes away. The talk should get back to the police and help to convince them. Or at least confuse them."

He looked at me shrewdly. "Don Milo, is it that you look for someone named Moreno?"

"Why?" I asked.

"Things I have heard in the police chief's office made me think this is so. As you said, it is better if I do not know this, but I wondered."

"What have you heard?"

"Nothing. Only vague suggestions."

"And why did you wonder?"

"If it is true," he said, "then I wish to tell you that the man named Moreno is dead."

"How do you know?"

"My mother's cousin," he said, "has a son who works on the burial detail in the prison of Santa Monica. He says they were called out at three in the morning not long ago to bury a prisoner, and he swears it was Moreno."

"Is he certain?"

He shrugged. "He says he is. He has nothing to gain by it. And he has told no one but the family. We have told no one else. One does not speak of such things in the Monican Republic."

"What about Alberto de la Garra?" I asked.

"The one who killed the American and then killed himself in the prison? I know nothing about him."

"Does your mother's cousin's son know if he killed himself or was killed?"

"He has not said," he answered. "Which means he does not know, for Bernardo tells to the family everything he knows. It is a family with much knowledge. If Don Milo is interested, we do know that de la Garra killed the American. He shot him through the head from behind."

"How do you know that?" I asked. "From the confession?"

He shook his head. "The confession, according to the newspapers, said that they had a fight. There was no fight. My sister's brother-in-law saw the killing."

"How?" I asked.

"He was sunning himself up north of the city. My sister's brother-in-law likes to take a siesta up there where the grass is tall. He saw the two men walking together, and de la Garra fell behind the American, then pulled a gun and shot him."

"Did he tell the police this?"

"Ca! Por supuesto que no!" he exclaimed. "In the Monican Republic one does not rush to the police with stories of what one has seen. One waits until the newspapers have published what it is that the police wish to say about the thing. Then, if one wishes, one goes to the police and says that it is so. But even that is sometimes dangerous. My uncle's oldest son once spent two months in prison for doing that. The police had changed their minds by the time he reached them."

"Well," I said dryly, "at least you seem to have a large family."

"Very large," he said. "Here is the next house, Don Milo."

In the next day or so I was to become glad that Luis had a large family. That day when I got back to the hotel I discovered there had been hundreds of phone calls and there were almost a hundred people waiting to see me. All in answer to the ad I'd run. It seemed that everybody in Puerto Torcido had antiques and family heirlooms. And they all wanted to show them to me.

More people and more phone calls arrived even as I was trying to cope with all this. The next morning it was worse. So I solved it by hiring two of Luis's cousins to see the people and make careful lists of what they had. And we arranged to route everyone to the home of one of the cousins.

In the meantime Luis and I went on visiting old homes outside of the city. And every night I saw Juana. We did the same things almost every night. Finally, I noticed that the policeman who followed each night was beginning to get bored. And Luis reported that Carnicero could hardly keep his eyes open while hearing about all the antiques we looked at each day.

The only other thing that happened was that Raimundo Perrola phoned me twice. Each time, after inquiring how I was doing with my search for the old manuscript and making sure there was nothing he could do to help, he got around to the main subject: had I assured Miss Mellany that they were doing everything to assist her representative? I kept telling him that I hadn't but that I would the first time I spoke to her. I guess he was getting anxious to secure a new wife.

After my fifth day, I had just about decided that even I

couldn't look at another antique. We had pretty well covered outlying old homes, so now I could switch to the city and maybe find out some other things. It wasn't one of my jobs, but I wanted to find out whether de la Garra had really committed suicide or not. I wanted to find out what had happened to the hundred and thirty thousand dollars that Moreno had withdrawn. And I had to start doing something about a plan for getting the manuscript out of the Palace. Not to mention a way to deliver the Chief of Police of Puerto Torcido into the hands of Lieutenant Johnny Rockland in New York. More of what Martin Raymond would have called small problems.

I went up to my hotel room the end of that fifth day and went through my usual ritual. First a hot shower, then a shave, and then some Canadian Club to take the taste of dust out of my mouth. I had a date with Juana again that night, but it was still two or three hours away. I stretched out across the bed with my drink and tried to apply myself to one of the stickiest problems: how to pick the pocket of a dictator. I had come prepared in a way—I had a manuscript to substitute for it—but I still couldn't just walk calmly in and switch them while Torcido was watching me. I'm pretty good at sleight of hand, but a manuscript is a little too large to palm.

The telephone rang.

I dragged myself off the bed and went over to answer it.

"Señor March?" a voice asked. It was a woman's voice. A nice one, warm and sexy. And, I thought, vaguely familiar.

"Yes," I said.

"I would like to see you as soon as possible," she said. "Could you meet me somewhere? I am Señorita Fulano."

That stopped me for a second. Fulano was the name the underground contact was supposed to give me. Juana was Señorita Fulano. And this was definitely not Juana. "Yes?" I said.

"Dichosos los ojos que ven a usted," she said, giving the sentence that was also supposed to identify the underground contacts. I was beginning to get knee-deep in contacts

"All right," I said. "Where shall I meet you?"

"Do you know the Café Bendito?"

"No, but I suppose I could find it."

"It's on Avenida Torcido," she said. "It will take you perhaps fifteen minutes to reach it from your hotel. I will meet you there in twenty-five minutes."

"All right," I said. "But how will I know you?"

She laughed softly. "You will know me," she said. There was a click as she hung up.

Great, I thought. They couldn't dig up any underground to fight Torcido, but for the visiting American the place was overflowing. Well, there was only one way to find out why. I got up and dressed. I made sure to remember to buckle on my holster and gun. Then I went downstairs and found a taxi and told him to take me to the Café Bendito.

SEVEN

The Café Bendito proved to be a small combination bar and restaurant. On the bar side, I saw as I entered, there were a number of curtained booths in the back. There were several men at the bar drinking, but no girls in sight. I was about to go look in the restaurant side when I heard something that sounded like a snake hissing. I looked around. The only person looking at me was the bartender, a rotund little man with one of the fiercest-looking mustaches I'd ever seen. Only on him it looked like a musical comedy prop.

"Ven aca," he said hoarsely.

He obviously meant me, so I went over. He leaned across the bar confidently. "You are the Señor March?" he asked in a stage whisper that carried farther than if he had spoken normally.

I admitted I was. There didn't seem to be anything to lose by that.

"The lady is in the farthest booth back," he said. "She is waiting for you. You would like something sent back?"

"Claro que sí," I said. "Send whatever the lady is drinking, and send me ... a brandy." That seemed about the safest thing to order. I would have preferred a martini, but this hardly seemed the place to order one. In fact, in most places a martini only serves to convince you that practically everybody owns stock in the vermouth companies.

I walked on back to the last booth. The curtains were drawn. I unbuttoned my coat and made sure it was loose just in case I had to get to my gun quickly.

She was right. I knew her. She was the little dark-haired girl who had come into my office with a pastel blue gun to shoot me. She was the girl who'd been on the plane with me. According to the Pan American records her last name was Sanjurjo. And now she was going to claim she was Fulano.

"Buenos tardes, Señor March," she said.

"Dichosos los ojos que ven a usted," I said. "Maybe it is a small world after all. What color gun are you going to use this time?"

"I am sorry about that," she said. "I will explain. That is also one of the reasons I wanted to see you. Won't you sit down? Please."

"Well, I did promise you another chance, didn't I?" I said. I slid into the booth opposite her. "You just have to give me a little time. I'm used to being shot at, but not by such pretty girls."

"I gave you a little time before," she said with a smile. "To smoke a cigarette. That was very clever of you. I'm glad that you stopped me from shooting you."

"So that you could try again down here?" I asked. "But you didn't have to do the Fulano bit. I'd have come even if you told me who you really were, Señorita Sanjurjo."

She looked surprised for a minute. "How—" she began. Then she smiled. "But of course. You got my name from the seating arrangement on the plane. But you were expecting someone named Fulano, weren't you?"

"Yes. But not so many of them."

"I know that I am the second," she said. "I will explain."

There was a discreet knock against the side of the booth.

"Come," I said.

The curtain parted and there was the bartender with two drinks. One was my brandy and the other was a tall glass filled with amber liquid and ice. He put them on the table and withdrew.

"What are you drinking?" I asked her.

"Vermouth and soda. I do not drink much."

"I can see that," I said in disgust. "Go ahead, honey. You were about to explain about almost shooting me and other small items."

"Did you ever hear of Felipe Sanjurjo?" she asked.

I shook my head.

"He is my brother. He is one of the most important members of whatever underground there is in the Monican Republic. He is the one who was originally supposed to come and see you. He was arrested two days before—even before the message arrived telling him to meet you."

"I heard that the man who was supposed to meet me had been arrested," I said. "The underground sent a girl in his place. And she wasn't you."

"I know," she said. "Let me tell it from the beginning. I was in school in the United States. I heard that my brother had been arrested and I also heard that Torcido had hired an American gunman to come to the Monican Republic. I'm afraid that I jumped to the conclusion that the two things were related. The name of the American gunman was Milo March."

"I'm flattered," I said.

"I was angry and frightened," she went on. "Torcido always seems to be able to buy so many people in other countries—especially the United States. Nice people. I thought that was what was happening again. And that this time it involved my brother. I had the gun, so I came looking for you."

She smiled. "I don't suppose I could have killed you, but I wanted to."

"I noticed," I said dryly.

"I knew something was wrong," she said, "when you accused me of working for El Nariz. But I didn't know what. I ran."

"You know El Nariz?"

"The name only. What Monican doesn't know it? He is the one who has killed so many of our people."

"Why didn't you tell me any of this on the plane?"

"Because I still didn't know who you were," she said. "It has taken me all of this time to get permission to visit my brother. I saw him in the prison yesterday. He has received word even in there and so he told me what he knows about it. I have not been near the other members of the underground because it would not be safe for them to be seen with Felipe's sister. My brother told me to come and see you and to use the name Fulano."

"What about the other Fulano?" I asked.

"Juana Ramos," she said. She spoke the name with scorn. "I know her. She is a member of the underground, but my brother does not trust her. He had nothing to do with her being appointed to take his place in meeting you. He believes that she works for Carnicero, the Chief of Police in Puerto Torcido."

"I've met the Chief," I said. "What makes your brother think that Juana works for him?"

"I do not know. He thinks so. He asked me to come and see you and to help in any way I can."

"I don't think it makes much difference," I said. "Almost everybody seems to work for Carnicero. Besides, I've told her nothing. Nor will I tell you. And so far as I can see, the underground can tell me nothing. All they seem to know is what they read in the newspapers."

"That is not true," she said. "Perhaps that is what the blond one tells you."

"Okay," I said. "What do you know about Moreno?"

She hesitated. "Not too much," she finally admitted. "My brother said to tell you that we know the American pilot brought someone here the day after Dr. Moreno was kidnapped in New York. The man was drugged. We believe it was Dr. Moreno, but no one saw his face. He was taken to an empty part of the prison and locked up. Nothing has been heard from him since. We also know that the American pilot had too much to drink one night in a café and bragged about how much he knew and that he never had to worry about losing his job. The next day he was killed."

"Do you know how he was killed?"

"They say in a fight, but that means nothing. Alberto de la Garra had been used many times before to kill people who were no longer useful. Always it was in a fight and always he was tried for the killing and freed. That is why we do not believe that he committed suicide as they say."

"But do you *know* that he didn't commit suicide?"

"No, we do not know it. But my brother is certain."

I thought about it for a minute. I wasn't buying anything just yet, but some of it sounded true. Certainly she had told me more than Juana had. I liked Juana, but that didn't mean she couldn't be working for Carnicero. For that matter, both girls could be.

"Prisoners always know everything that goes on in a prison," I said. "Can't your brother find out what happened to de la Garra?"

She shook her head. "Political prisoners are kept in one part of the prison and the criminals in another. He was locked up in the criminal side. There is no way for there to be communication between the two sections."

"What is going to happen to your brother?"

"I do not know. He thinks they will hold him for a while and then turn him loose. This has happened several times. They have nothing on him but suspicion, and it is a cat-and-mouse game they have long played with him. But one can never tell when they will tire of the game and shoot. They do not need a reason."

"What about you?" I asked. "Have you worked in the underground?"

"I did before," she said. "Then I went to the United States to go to school. My brother has kept me up with what is going on, and sometimes I meet with those of us who are in New York. Why?"

"I just wondered. Do you know a man in Puerto Torcido named Luis Argensola?"

"There are many Argensolas here," she said. She thought

a minute. "Is that the one who drives a taxi? If so, he works for the police."

"That's the one."

"He is an opportunist," she said scornfully. "He will do anything for money."

"Maybe your underground ought to cultivate a few opportunists," I said gently. "He seems to know more about what is going on than any of you do. ... What's your full name?"

"Elena Sanjurjo."

"Okay, Elena. Maybe everything you say is true. I'll play along and see. But I'm just as suspicious as your people are. I have a job to do down here and I'm going to do it even if somebody has to get hurt. And I'm going to try to keep that somebody from being me. In the meantime, I'm willing to listen to anybody who wants to talk to me—whether I believe them or not. Understand?"

"Yes," she said in a small voice.

"I may want to ask you some questions," I said. "Where can I meet you tomorrow night?"

"Here, if you like," she said.

"Same time?"

She nodded.

"Está bien, Elena," I said. I finished my brandy. "I will see you tomorrow night. Do you think it's safe for me to turn my back on you?" I grinned at her.

"That's not fair," she said. "I explained it to you."

"Sure you did, honey." I got up, parted the curtains, and left. On the way out I stopped and paid the bartender. He scowled at me as if I had committed a terrible sin by staying with such a pretty girl only long enough to buy her one drink. I was inclined to agree with him, but I left anyway.

I met Juana and we went out on the town. I didn't mention anything about my other meeting or try to ask her any questions. There would be plenty of time for that. In the meantime, she wasn't learning anything from me, so it didn't make too much difference if she did work for the police.

Luis was around the next morning at his usual time. We'd gotten into the habit of stopping in a little café for coffee every morning as we started out, and we did the same this morning.

"More houses again today, Don Milo?" he asked in a resigned tone as we were served our coffee.

"I don't think so, Luis," I said. "I think today we will help your cousin. We will get the names and addresses of some of the people who have answered the ad and we'll go around and see them, instead of waiting for them to come to us."

He groaned. "It will be just as bad. Who can stand to look at such junk? It is enough to turn a man into a Communist."

"Better not let Carnicero hear you say that," I said.

He turned pale and looked around the café. "You see what you have done to me, Don Milo? I, who could always walk between the devil and the fire without getting singed, am suddenly becoming careless. *Dios mío!*"

"It's all right, Luis," I said, grinning at him. "The Communists wouldn't have you. They have no room for poets either. You know anything about a guy named Felipe Sanjurjo?"

"*Claro que sí,*" he said. "He is the head of the revolutionary group against Torcido. At least, that is what they say. Nobody has ever proved it. He is in prison now. Here, proof is not necessary."

"What do you know about him?"

"That he is a fool. Once he and his family had much money. Torcido has taken everything away from him, but still he fights. Against what? Shadows. So, he is a fool."

"Know anything about his sister?"

"Oh, that one," he said, giving me a knowing look. "She is also a fool, but a pretty one, which makes a difference. You are a sly one, Don Milo. You have been here only a few days and already you know the prettiest women. But the Sanjurjo girl is something different. You know what you must do, Don Milo?"

"What must I do?" I asked.

"First make her fall in love with you," he said seriously. "She is that kind of woman. Then ..." He shrugged. "You remember what Juan Ruiz said: *'La niña que amores ha, sola cómo dormira?'* "he said. " 'The girl who is in love, how shall she sleep alone?' "

"Luis," I said, laughing, "you are a born *chulo*. You have really missed your calling. What I was trying to ask was if his sister was also part of the revolutionary group."

"Sometimes," he said, shrugging.

"What about Juana Ramos?" I asked. "Does she work for the police?"

He looked startled, then thoughtful. "I do not know, Don Milo," he said finally. "I had not thought of it, but it is possible. She would be the ideal type. As a dancer she could easily meet many men. Perhaps."

"Okay, let's go to work," I said. *"Vámonos ahora."*

"Voy," he said.

We started. At each house, Luis stayed in the car and I went in alone. I looked at the family heirlooms and talked. I always managed to steer the conversation around to Moreno and the death of the American pilot and the suicide of his killer. But it was a waste of time. Either they were all ignorant of what had happened or they were frightened. Perhaps a little of each.

Finally, by midmorning, I'd had all I could stand. I'd noticed that there was no police tail on us, and I decided to hell with it. It was time I started doing something more constructive than looking at old Spanish pots and costumes. One idea had been working through my head even as I looked and talked. I was bored with playing games. I wanted some action.

"Basta, ya," I said to Luis as I came out of the fourth house. "I've had it. What's the name of your mother's cousin's son, or whatever he is? The one that digs graves."

"Bernardo," he said. He looked at me curiously. "Why?"

"I want to go talk to him."

"He may not want to talk to you."

"He will if you tell him to," I said. "And you'll tell him to—for twenty-five dollars a day."

He started the motor and pulled away from the curb. "Don Milo," he said gloomily, "you are making me nervous. It has been so for the past two days now."

"What am I doing to make you nervous?" I asked.

"It is not what you do; it is what boils within you. I know men like you, Don Milo. You plan everything carefully and you go along with the plan, then—poof—you are bored and you become like the bull when the cape has been waved in his face."

I laughed. "Don't worry about me, Luis. This is planning, too."

"I do not worry about you," he said gloomily. "I worry about myself, Luis Argensola. I am a poet, not a hero."

"You are neither," I told him. "You are a businessman. You are worried about your twenty-five dollars a day from me, your ten dollars a day from the taxi, and your fifty dollars a month from the police. If you can hold on to all three long enough, you will be richer than Torcido."

"Not so loud," he said. "If Torcido should hear you, he might take all three jobs away from me and do them himself."

"I believe you. Which brings me to something I want to ask you. Do you know anything about Torcido?"

"Only what one hears, Don Milo. He does not make friends with taxi drivers."

"Outside of power and money," I said, "what is important to Torcido?"

"To live so that he may enjoy his power and money."

"No, I mean is there anything in his life that will make him drop everything else for the moment and come running?"

He thought for a minute. "It is said that he is so fond of his youngest son there is nothing he will not do for the boy. It is said that when he gets a letter from that son, he will interrupt the most important meeting to read it."

"Where is his youngest son?"

"In the United States. He goes to a military school there, but I do not know where. It is said that the youngest son is to succeed Torcido when he dies."

"Okay," I said. I tucked the information away for later use.

"Don Milo," Luis said, "why do you wish to talk to Bernardo? To ask him about the man he says was Moreno?"

"No," I said. "I expect that Bernardo is right about that. I want to ask him some questions about the prison."

"What kind of questions?"

"I am about to become terribly interested in prison reform," I said.

He looked at me reproachfully. "You do not trust me."

"With my life," I said. "Up to a point. You will hear the questions when I ask them of Bernardo."

He kept quiet and drove. We were soon stopping before a small house in the outskirts of the city. We got out of the car and went up to the door. Luis knocked. After an interval the door was opened and a tall, stooped, gloomy-looking man stared out. He exchanged greetings with Luis without any change of expression. Luis introduced us. This was Bernardo. He invited us into the house and offered us some coffee.

"Don Milo," Luis said when we were drinking the coffee, "is from the United States. He is interested in prisons and wishes to ask you some questions about the prison of Santa Monica. You may speak freely before him."

"Why not ask at the prison, then?" Bernardo asked. "Surely they know more about it than I do."

"I will carry out investigations there, too," I said, "but I'd like to ask you some questions. After all, you have a slightly different view of it."

"The graves are well cared for," he said. "And I will bet they have more graves than almost any other prison."

"Do they put markers on them?" I asked. I wasn't really

interested, but I wanted to get the conversation started.

"No markers, only numbers. I am told that in the office they have a chart showing who is buried at each number."

That gave me an idea. "Do you recall the number of the grave of the man you thought was Dr. Moreno?"

Bernardo glanced briefly at Luis, but that was his only reaction. "Yes," he said. "It was two thousand nine hundred and fifty-seven."

I made a mental note of the number. "Now," I said, "do you think you could draw me a rough plan of the prison?"

He shrugged. "Perhaps," he said. He went to get paper and pencil while Luis sat there looking unhappy. Bernardo returned and labored over the paper, chewing his upper lip and gripping the pencil as though it were trying to get away from him. Finally he finished. He stared at it a minute and seemed satisfied. He pushed the paper toward me. "Here you are, Señor," he said.

He had drawn what looked like a fat V with a circle around it.

"The circle," he explained, coming over to me, "is the wall around the prison. The gates are here in the front. This part of the prison"—he pointed to the left arm of the V—"is where they keep the political prisoners. The criminals are kept in the other section. In the center is where the prisoners exercise. On either side of the prison are the graveyards. Even in death the politicos are kept apart from the others. The entrance to the prison is here." He pointed to the bottom of the V.

"That is the only entrance?" I asked.

"*Sí.* The only main entrance. There are little doors through which we carry the dead. They are here and here." He pointed to each side of the V, down near the bottom.

"Where are the offices?"

"Around the main entrance."

"How does one get from one part of the prison to the other?"

"Only through the offices, Señor."

"Bernardo," I said, "when you helped to bury the man you thought was Moreno, from which part of the prison did he come?"

"The political."

"Did you also help to bury Alberto de la Garra?"

"The one who killed the American pilot? Yes. He came from the criminal side."

"How had he died?" I asked.

"Strangled. He had hanged himself in his cell. His neck was twisted to one side. It was not pretty."

"Death is never pretty," I said. "Here around the prison, Bernardo, where are the guards?"

"At the gate."

"Only at the gate? Not along the walls?"

"No. They are not needed along the walls. In all the history of the Fortress of Santa Monica, no one has ever escaped from it." He said it with a kind of pride. He might not approve of what went on in the prison, but since he was associated with it, it was good that it was a strong prison.

"And inside?" I asked.

"They patrol inside. But that is mostly to stop disturbances. No one has ever escaped."

"At night, too?"

"At night, too."

"What about the office at night?" I asked.

"There is a night warden there. That is all. But prisoners come in at night, and many are carried out at night. He is there."

"One more question, Bernardo. What about the locks at the prison?"

"They are formidable, Señor."

"I'm sure they are," I said. "But do you know what kind they are?"

He shrugged. "They are modern, I think. And strong."

"Are they electric?"

He thought for a minute. "I do not think so. They are opened with keys."

"The side doors, too?"

"Sí."

"Are there any bars across the side doors on the inside?"

He thought again. "No. Only the locks. But they are very strong locks. No one could break them."

"Le agradezo mucho su amabilidad, Bernardo," I said, getting up.

"De nada," he said. "Luis always has friends who ask questions about everything. If it is not one, it is another. Once he even brought someone who wanted to know how to dig a grave."

We said our good-byes and prepared to leave. At the door, I thanked Bernardo again.

"De nada," he repeated. *"Aquí está usted como en casa."*

Luis and I got in the car and drove away. He glanced at me.

"Don Milo," he said, "is it that you are thinking of trying to get Felipe Sanjurjo out of the prison?"

"No, Luis," I said. "I am thinking of something else. I will tell you in good time. ... Luis, Carnicero told me that there were no criminals in the Monican Republic. Is that true?"

"There are some," he said cautiously. "Why?"

"My interest in prison reform," I said. "Where in Puerto Torcido would such criminals go if they wished to obtain tools for their trade?"

"I do not understand."

"Yes, you do. If a Monican criminal wanted to break into a store and rob it, where would he go to get the tools needed?"

"Am I supposed to know everything?" he exclaimed.

"I'm beginning to think perhaps you do," I said. "I've been paying you twenty-five dollars a day for doing nothing. Now it is time you started earning your money."

He sighed heavily. "You are a difficult man, Don Milo. And you make me nervous. Sometimes I think you are paying me only so that I may buy a coffin. ... The husband of my father's sister has a store where he sells the implements to farmers and carpenters. In the back room he sells more delicate implements. I will take you there."

He drove a meandering route through the city. I knew that this was partly to make sure that no one was following us, but it was partly so that I would not know where we were going. Finally he pulled to a stop in front of a small store, which I suspected was not far from the spot where we'd started.

"Come," he said gloomily.

I followed him into the store. There was only one man in

there, sitting behind the counter. He was enormously fat, with a round, beaming face. On his upper lip there was a mustache so tiny that it was ridiculous. He was reading a book and he looked up, marking his place with a pudgy forefinger.

Luis introduced us. The man's name was Miguel Anchura.

"I am pleased to know you, Señor," he said. "Business is slow today. I was reading the story of Don Quixote. It is a great book."

"He is always reading it," Luis said. "It is the only book he has ever read. It is the only one he will ever read. As soon as he finishes it, he starts all over again on the first page."

"It is a great book," the man explained.

"Don Milo wishes to talk to you in the back room," Luis said.

"Surely," the man said politely. He put a match in the book to mark his place and got up. He waddled toward the back of the store. We followed him.

"Now, Señor," he said when we were in the back room, "how may I be honored by serving you?"

"I am looking for something special," I told him. "A set of steel picks—pieces of steel in various sizes which, in the right hands, will open any lock in the world."

He pursed his fat mouth until it looked like a rosebud. "You are in luck, Señor. There was a German here, oh, five or six years ago. He came with the thought of robbing the home of the Benefactor. He was arrested before he succeeded and was given twenty-four hours to leave the country. In some mysterious way, his money had vanished while he was in the police station. So he sold me everything he had in order to obtain money to leave. He owned such a set as you mention. Made of the finest German steel. I have never been able to sell it because it costs too much for poor Monicans." He looked me over very carefully. "It is quite expensive."

"How much?"

"One hundred pesos. The Monican peso is worth the same as your dollars, Señor."

"I know," I said. "If the set is what you say it is, I'll pay your price."

He smiled and walked across the room and threw open the lid of a large wooden chest. As far as I could see, it seemed to be filled with a jumble of such things as nuts and bolts and wire, but his hand went unerringly beneath the junk and came up with a small roll of velvet cloth. He came back to me, unrolling it, then handed it over. He was right. It was as fine a set of picks as I'd ever seen. I gave him his money.

"From what I've seen of Puerto Torcido and especially the Argensola family," I said, "everyone has a talent for working both sides of the street. I trust that news of my purchase will not reach the ears of the police. I can see where one might do a profitable business selling something and then buying it back at half price a day or two later."

He smiled. "At this price, have no fear," he said. "It carries with it what you might call a guarantee. For a lesser price— well, who knows?"

"Okay," I said. "Let's go, Luis."

We went back out through the store. The last I saw of Miguel Anchura, he was again picking up his book and opening it.

"If I don't finish this job soon," I said to Luis as we got into the car, "the entire Argensola family, large as it is, will be able to retire and go to the United States and write poetry."

"Should you give your business to strangers?" he asked. "It is unthinkable."

"I could think about it if I had a chance," I said. "Well, let's call it a day for now, Luis. You can take me back to the hotel and then pick me up later tonight."

He was silent on the drive back. When we reached the hotel and I was getting out, he said, "Where do we go tonight, Don Milo?"

"I like to drive at night," I said cheerfully. "It's relaxing. If I think of some specific place I want to go, I'll tell you tonight. Do you know where the Café Bendito is?"

He nodded.

"Okay, pick me up there at about nine o'clock. *Hasta luego.*"

"*Está bien,*" he said unhappily, and drove away.

I went upstairs and had a couple of drinks. Then I took a shower and stretched out on the bed. It was apt to be a rugged night. I went quickly to sleep and slept for a couple of hours. I got up and shaved. I had another drink and ordered some food sent up. While I was eating, I thought about the case. Slowly, I was beginning to get some ideas about how to work it. I didn't especially like the ideas, but there wasn't going to be any easy way to do this one.

The phone rang. It was Perrola wanting to know again if I'd told Miss Mellany how much he was knocking himself out for her. I told him again that I hadn't but that I most surely would. There was no point lying to him about it. If I had made any phone call outside of Puerto Torcido, I was sure he would have known about it within five minutes. But I was glad he was still dangling on the hook. That was going to be part of my plan.

Later I phoned Juana and told her I wouldn't see her that night. She wanted to know what I was going to do, and I explained that I had to look at some antiques and I would call her the next day. I hung up before she could get more curious. Then it was time to go meet Elena. I got dressed and went downstairs. I took a taxi to the café.

The bartender was happy to see me. I began to wonder if he was a marriage broker on the side. He indicated that I was to go on back to the last booth. I did so and Elena was there, nursing a vermouth and soda.

"Do you live here in this booth?" I asked.

She smiled. "It is just that I believe in being prompt," she said.

"An admirable habit," I said, "which I never acquired."

There was a knock on the booth and the curtains parted to reveal that the bartender had brought me a brandy without being told to. My opinion of him went up.

"Have you decided yet who to believe?" she asked.

"I believe everybody," I said generously. "That way nobody will get his feelings hurt. Did you visit your brother in the prison?"

"Yes."

"I know, of course," I said, "that you must have seen him in the visiting room, but do you have a rough idea of where his cell is in the prison?"

"Yes," she said. She looked at me curiously. "He said he

was in a cell on the second floor in about the middle of the wing. Why?"

"I'm a collector of useless information," I said lightly. I pulled out the rough plan Bernardo had drawn for me and put it on the table. I pointed with my finger. "You'd say about here, on the second floor?"

"I guess," she said. "Why do you want to know?"

"I told you."

"Are you thinking of trying to rescue him from the prison?" she asked. There was a note of excitement in her voice.

"I don't even know if he wants to be rescued," I said. "Besides, I'm not in that line of business. I was just curious. But I am going to try to talk to your brother tonight."

"I don't think they will let you," she said. "Nobody else has been permitted to see him, and it was very difficult for me to get permission."

"They'll let me," I said. "Any message you want me to give him for you?"

"Just tell him that I pray for him every day," she said.

"Sure," I said. I picked up the drawing and studied it for a couple of minutes. Then I put a match to it and let it burn up in the ashtray. When it was burned, I used my thumb to grind the charred pieces into dust.

"If you are going to try to rescue Felipe," she said, "perhaps some members of the underground would help."

"I'm not going to rescue anyone," I said. "Now let's talk of other things."

"What?"

"You, for instance."

We did, but I didn't learn much. She was going to school on a scholarship and what little money they had left. She wanted to finish school and come back to help her brother fight Torcido, but her brother was opposed to the idea. That was about all. Anything more personal went unanswered.

Finally it was nine o'clock. I arranged to meet her the same place the next night and left. Luis was waiting in the car outside. I climbed in beside him.

"Where do we go, Don Milo?" he asked politely. I grinned to myself. He was being polite to show that he was hurt because I had not confided in him.

"Oh, just drive around," I said. "Anywhere—as long as we go by someplace where we can borrow a ladder."

"A ladder?" he said. *"Dios mío.* What do you plan to do?"

"I thought all Spanish people were romantic," I said. "You should jump to the conclusion that I want it to climb to the window of some pretty girl."

"Claro que sí," he said sarcastically. He wanted to see if I would volunteer any more information. When I didn't, he sighed. "I have a ladder at home. We will stop and get it."

He turned off the main avenue and after a while stopped in front of a small, dark house. He went inside and was soon back with a folding ladder that fit into the back of the car. He climbed behind the steering wheel and waited for orders.

"Now," I said, "we will drive to the Fortress of Santa Monica."

"Qué diablos," Luis said. "It is as I feared. You are going to try to rescue that revolutionary. It is madness, Don Milo."

"I don't know why everybody thinks I'm so big-hearted," I

said. "I am not going to try to rescue anyone. As a poet, Luis, you should appreciate what I am going to do. I intend to break into the prison of Santa Monica."

"*Válgame Dios!*" he exclaimed. "It is worse than I feared. You have been robbed of your senses. Why should anyone break into a prison? If you are so anxious, almost any policeman will escort you."

"I prefer my way," I said. "*Vámonos ahora,* Luis."

He started the motor and the car pulled away from the curb.

"Be sure we are not followed," I said.

"Do you think I too am a fool?" he asked bitterly. "I want to live even if you don't. But you, Don Milo, hourly diminish my chances to do so."

"You worry too much, Luis," I said. "I increase your chances to live by making you rich so that you may go to the United States and write poetry."

"Riches," he said bitterly. He made a right-hand turn, then quickly one to the left. "As Jorge Manrique said, '*Los plazeres y dulcores de esta vida trabajada que tenemos, qué son sino corredores, y la muerte la celada en que caemos?*' " he said. " 'The pleasure and sweetness of this toiling life we lead, what are they but fleeting, and is not death the snare into which we fall?' "

"True," I said. "But enough poetry for now. Listen to me carefully, Luis. When we near the prison, turn off your lights and then stop somewhere near the wall. You will wait until I am over the top of the wall, then you will take your ladder and go home. And forget that you even saw me this night."

"It is my greatest wish that I had never seen you," he said.

"Except when you get your twenty-five dollars each day," I suggested.

"Except then," he admitted.

"Which brings me to the next point," I said. "Tonight I am not going to give you your pay. I will give it to you tomorrow."

"*Caray!* What if there is no tomorrow for you?"

"There will be. I merely want to be sure that you have a personal interest in my return. By tomorrow I will owe you fifty dollars. Now, I want you to go to the hotel in the morning and wait for me. If I am not there by noon, you are to phone the American Ambassador and tell him where I am. He will then get me out. But I do not think that will be necessary. Now, do you understand?"

"I understand that you do not trust me," he said.

"As far as a dollar bill will reach," I said cheerfully. "Are we not practically brothers? Did we not almost die together on the mountainside? But you do understand?"

"I understand. *Caray!* It would be better if I did not even hear. For men such as I, ears are a curse. But I will do as you say, Don Milo."

"Good."

Another few minutes and I could see the prison, rearing against the sky like an old castle, ahead of us. Luis turned off his lights and a minute later switched off the motor and let the car coast. We were on a small side street with no other traffic. A few more yards and he brought the car to a halt within the shadow of the prison wall. He climbed out and helped me place the ladder against the wall.

"*Buena suerte,* Don Milo," he whispered.

"Hasta luego, Luis," I said. I turned and went up the ladder. When I reached the top, I quickly dropped over on the other side without looking back. I crouched down against the wall until I heard him start the car and drive away.

I'd made the first step. I was inside the prison wall.

EIGHT

I waited until a few minutes after Luis had left, then started across the grounds toward the prison. There were no lights on the grounds at all. I could see a few lights in the prison and there were lights at the gate. That was all. I would have liked having a flashlight, but I had known it would be too risky using one. I stumbled across the dark ground as best I could.

From the way we had approached, I knew I was on the side where the political wing was, which was good. I wanted to talk to Felipe Sanjurjo for a few minutes. I didn't think there was much he could tell me, but since I was going inside, I might as well find out.

It must have taken me more than a half hour to cross the prison compound, inching across it the way I did, but presently I was up against the massive stone of the prison itself. I seemed to be somewhere in the middle. I got my bearings by locating the gates and then felt my way along the wall in that direction. Again it was slow going, for I could see nothing and I didn't want to stumble over something. I had no way of knowing where the guards might be, and any sound might carry to them.

Finally, however, I came to what was unquestionably a door. From Bernardo's description, it must be the door through which they carried the dead to bury them. It was a huge iron door, with a small peephole near the top. I looked through and could see a dimly lit corridor. It was empty.

I got out my set of steel picks and went to work on the door. It was a tough job, partly because it was a long time since I had worked on a lock. But at last I felt the tumblers move, and a moment later the door swung open. I breathed a sigh of relief at finding they were at least efficient enough to keep the door oiled. It made no sound as it opened.

I slipped inside quickly and closed it so that no one would see a telltale beam of light on the outside. I stayed close to the door and looked around. Ahead stretched a long, gleaming corridor with nothing in sight but the walls and the light. Somewhere off in the distance I could hear the murmur of voices. That was good. It meant that sounds carried well in here and that I could have advance warning of anyone approaching. Every few feet along the corridor there were cutoffs, so that there would also be a chance to dodge a patrol if one came along. And with the building carrying sounds as it did, I would know well enough ahead of time. That's one good thing, I thought, about all policemen; they wear heavy shoes and walk heavily enough to let you know when they are near.

I went silently down the long corridor, listening and watching. I unbuttoned my coat so that it would be easy to get to the gun. According to the crude drawing I'd had, I was on the ground floor of the political wing of the prison. I wanted to get to the second floor. I kept watching for a stairway. Finally, at the third cutoff, I found it.

A set of iron stairs, going up. I stood at the corner for a

minute, listening. There was no sound. I went quickly up the stairs.

On the second floor, there was another long corridor, running at right angles to one I'd been in on the ground floor. On each side there was a series of doors with iron bars. The floor was quiet, the cells all dark. But I'd been in prisons before, especially Spanish prisons; I knew that all along that silent row there were men lying with their eyes open in the dark, thinking and scheming. Knowing this, I could almost feel their thoughts. I stayed for a moment at the top step of the stairs, feeling the thoughts and listening for the footsteps of a guard. All was silence.

After a while, I moved down the corridor as quietly as I could. As I passed the cells, I knew there were eyes watching me, but there was no sign that anyone saw me. I went along until I thought I was somewhere near the center of the cell block. I stopped in front of a cell. *"Dónde está Felipe Sanjurjo?"* I asked softly.

There was a moment of silence. Then: "Two cells down. On this side. *Cuidado.*" It came in a whisper.

I walked along to the second cell door. I stopped beside it and waited a minute.

There was no sound of footsteps anywhere along the corridor. All I could hear was the breathing in the cell before which I stood. There was a waiting, watchful quality about it. Then, as I waited, I understood why. I heard the faint tap somewhere inside on the wall and knew that even as I had walked there, the prisoner two cells away had been busy passing the message that someone was looking for Sanjurjo by tapping on the wall of his neighbor. The neighbor passed it along to the next one, and so on. As I arrived at his cell, Sanjurjo was getting it from his neighbor. I waited until the taps had stopped.

"If you've gotten the message, Felipe," I said quietly, "I'm the guy who's looking for you." There was no immediate answer. "Felipe Sanjurjo?" I said.

"Yes?" a voice answered from the darkness of the cell.

"I am Milo March," I said. "From the United States. *Dichosos los ojos que ven a usted.*"

There was another moment of silence. "How are you here?" the voice then asked.

"I came in," I said. "First, do you have a cellmate?"

"Yes, but he is to be trusted."

"How often does the guard go by?"

"Every thirty minutes. He is due again before too long."

"All right," I said. I moved until I was standing directly in front of the cell door. I took the picks, separated one slender piece of steel, and went to work on the lock.

"What does he do as he passes through the corridor?"

"Shines a flash into each cell. That is all unless he sees something wrong."

"What do you have? One bed above the other?"

"No. A single bed on each side of the cell. Why?"

"I like to know what's around if anything happens," I said. "I saw your sister about an hour ago, Felipe."

"Yes? What did she say?"

"That she prayed for you every day. She thought I was coming to rescue you. I told her I wasn't. ... Do you want to be rescued?"

There was another silence. "No," he said finally. "I think they will let me go within a few days and that will be better. If I escaped, I would always be on the run. But how did you get in here? No one has ever broken out of Santa Monica since it was built."

"I know," I said dryly. "But it's always easier to break into jail than it is to break out. Have you learned anything about Moreno since you've been in here?"

"No," he said. "There was a prisoner brought in here about the right time, but no one ever saw him. He was kept upstairs where the cells are all empty. But he was heard screaming at night for a couple of nights. Then no more. It may have been Moreno."

"One of the gravediggers says it was," I said. "He claims that he helped to bury Moreno. I will try to check on it while I'm here."

Somewhere down the corridor a prisoner began singing. It was a love ballad.

"That means a guard is coming," Felipe said. "You had better run."

"No," I said. I had just felt the tumblers give beneath the probing steel in my hand. "If you don't mind, I'll come inside instead." I opened the cell door and stepped inside, pulling the door shut behind me. It would stay closed without being locked. "If you'll give me a hint how to find it, I'll hide under one of the beds until the guard passes. That's better than running."

"*Caray,*" whispered a strange voice. "He opened the door as though it had no lock and walked through."

"Here," said the other voice I had come to identify as belonging to Felipe. A hand touched my arm, guiding me. "You are very clever."

The hand guided me to the bed, then let go. I got down on the floor and crawled beneath the bed.

"Not clever," I said. "Prepared."

"It is the same thing. You are the man Elena was going to shoot in New York?"

"Yes."

"She told me about it. You are clever, Señor. Elena is not easily tricked, and she is an excellent shot. Now, quiet. The guard is getting near."

I could hear the footsteps myself. They grew louder, and then almost before I knew it, there was a light shining into the cell. It swept around in a semicircle, then winked away. The footsteps began to recede. When I could no longer hear them I came out from under the bed.

"What else have you learned, Señor?" Felipe asked.

"Not much," I admitted. "They tried to kill me in New York before I left. El Nariz. So I was marked for it down here. I've spent most of the time confusing them. They still try to watch everything I do, but they are not sure whether to kill me or not. But the honeymoon won't last forever, and now I go to work. I do know who El Nariz is."

"Who?" he asked fiercely.

"No," I said. "I promised a New York cop first crack at him. I'm going to try to get him back to New York. If that doesn't work out, I'll let you know. ... What about Juana Ramos?"

"I am certain she works for Carnicero, but I have never been able to prove it. Once, when she was very young, she was Torcido's mistress for a short time. She claims that is why she hates him and joined the underground, but I do not think so. Still, there are others who trust her. That is why she was able to get them to send her in my place. But be careful."

"I'm always careful," I said. "What did they arrest you for?"

"Suspicion. But I have been thinking since I have been in here, and it may be that they did it because they knew that you were coming. If that is true, they will let me go when you leave."

"Then I'll try to hurry it up," I told him. "Know anything about Perrola?"

"Nothing we can prove. We believe that he is the one who plans such things as the kidnapping of Moreno and the killing of Monican refugees. He has always performed important services for Torcido. And, Señor, do not be fooled by the clothes and the women and the manners of Perrola. He is clever and ruthless."

"No se fíe usted de él, es muy doble," said the other voice.

"I know," I said. "Now, look … my chief reason for breaking in here is that I want to find out how de la Garra died. The ones who will know are the prisoners in the cell block where he was kept. But they are not apt to talk to a stranger, even one who can break into the prison. Do you know anyone in that wing of the prison?"

"I do not," Felipe said. "Jorge?"

"No," said his cellmate. There was a moment of silence. "Perhaps Rafael," he suggested.

"Just the one," said Felipe. "We will ask him."

"Who is Rafael?" I asked.

"One of us. He has also spent some time in the other wing." He began to pound on the wall of the cell with his shoe. He was using Morse code, asking someone in the next cell to pass the question along to Rafael.

We waited, and after a few minutes the answer came back. He did know someone. Manuel Neruda, who had been on the third floor for two years and would be for another three.

"Ask him," I said, "if he will give me a note to this Manuel Neruda."

"There are no papers and pencils in here," Felipe said.

"I have paper and a pencil."

The tapping began again, a longer message this time, telling him who I was and what I wanted. We waited again and then the answer came. Yes.

"It is the fifth cell from here," Felipe said.

"Está bien," I said. I opened the cell door and looked out. There were no guards in sight. I stepped outside and closed the door. "I'd better lock you in again, so there will be no suspicion," I said.

"Of course."

It took only a minute to lock the door and then I walked down to the fifth cell. I stopped in front of it, close to the door. "Rafael?" I said.

"Sí," a voice answered from the dark cell. "You have the paper and pencil?"

I took them from my pocket and passed them through. A hand appeared to take them. A moment later a match was lit and in its flickering light I saw a thin little man bent over the paper on the floor, laboriously writing. When that match flickered out, another was lit. A few seconds later, it was blown out and the paper and pencil were handed back to me.

"There, Señor," the voice said. "Remember it is the third floor. Manuel Neruda. *Buena suerte.*"

I started back along the corridor. By this time everyone along one side of the cell block knew who I was and why I was there. As I passed each cell there came a whispered *"Buena suerte."* Good luck.

I went down the stairs carefully. When I reached the bottom, I stood at the corner and checked the other corridor. There was no one in sight. I could hear footsteps to the left, but they were going away. A few feet from where I stood, another corridor cut off of the main one into what looked as if it might be the offices. I crossed to it and looked. About half-way down there was an open door with light spilling out of it. I went down the corridor quietly, staying close to the wall and ready for action. When I reached the open door, I took a quick look inside. It was a small office, with one man in it. He was sitting with his feet on the desk, a steaming mug of coffee beside him, and was reading a paperback book.

When I was sure he was immersed in his book, I slipped quickly past the open door and went on down the corridor, stopping to look at each door. Finally I found the one I was looking for. Lettered on it was the word for Warden. I tried the door. It was locked. I brought out my thin slivers of steel and went to work. This was a simpler lock and it gave within a couple of minutes. I stepped inside and closed the door.

This office was in the front of the prison, and light from

the gate filtered through the window. Enough so that I could make out most objects in the room.

I had no idea where to look for what I wanted, so I began with the banks of filing cabinets, looking only at the headings on each folder. An hour later I had finally worked my way around to the big desk without finding anything. I was feeling pretty much like giving up, but I stuck with it. Then I found it, in one of the drawers of the desk. A thick, bound folder. On the front was the simple legend: *Sepulturas*. Graves.

I carried it over to the window where there was more light and looked through it. There was nothing in it but numbers and names. Well toward the back I found the number 2957. Opposite it was the name Jaime Moreno. Bernardo had been right. I took the folder back and replaced it. Then I left the office, locking the door behind me, and went back down the corridor. When I reached the small office, the man was still reading his book, smoking a brown-papered cigarette. I slipped past his door and when I reached the main corridor turned toward the other wing of the prison.

When I was almost to the stairway, I heard someone coming. The footsteps advanced with the steady rhythm of a guard marching on his post. I ducked into a cutoff and stood tightly against the wall. I took the gun from my holster and held it loosely, waiting.

The footsteps pounded nearer, then suddenly he came into view, a slightly fat figure in a rumpled blue uniform. A heavy gun swung on his hip. He marched stolidly by without looking anywhere except straight ahead. I let my breath out softly and eased the gun back into the holster. I waited until I could no longer hear the footsteps, then looked out. The way was clear. I went quickly up the stairs.

When I reached the top, I hesitated long enough to look at the note. It was addressed to Manuel Neruda and merely said that I was a *norteamericano* who could be trusted. It was signed Rafael Andrade, and beside the signature there was a curious and meaningless little drawing that was probably some sort of thieves' code. I folded the note and went on to the third floor. The corridor there, too, was deserted. I walked along it, again aware that I was being watched from the dark, barred caves on either side. But the only sound was the faint scuff of my feet on the concrete. I picked a cell at random and stopped in front of it.

"Manuel Neruda?" I asked softly.

"Why?" a voice asked.

"I came to tell him his car and chauffeur are at the door," I said. "Where do I find him?"

"Try at the seventh cell." There was a grin in the voice—and curiosity. As I started to walk, I heard the quick thumping on the wall.

At the seventh cell I stopped. "Manuel Neruda," I said.

"What do you want?" The invisible inmate asked. I held the note through the bars, and after a minute a hand reached for it. Inside the cell a match was struck and then shielded by a hand so that it showed only the note. A moment later it was extinguished.

"What do you want, *norteamericano?*" the voice asked. It was a hard voice, as though the throat had been baked too long in hot fires. And in it, too, I could hear the curiosity. This was a different prison than the other wing; here as quickly as they knew that someone had entered illegally, they would thirst to know how. Perhaps if one came in, one could go out.

"There was a man in here not long ago," I said, "who died here. I want to know how."

"Many die here, *norteamericano.* They die in many ways."

"This one was named Alberto de la Garra. He was not the usual inmate."

"That one," the voice said. There was the sound of spitting. "Talk to Pablo Vallejo. They were cellmates."

"Where do I find Pablo?" I asked.

"Go back five cells."

I turned and started back, the thumping on the walls accompanying me. This time the message was for Pablo and it was telling him that Rafael the Eel had said I was to be trusted and that I wanted to talk to him. It was being received in the fifth cell as I arrived. I stood close to the door and waited. While I waited, I used the steel picks. By the time the message was finished, I had the lock picked.

"Who are you, Señor?" a voice asked from the cell. It was the voice of an old man, tired and a little rusty from not being used too much.

"My name does not matter," I said. "I am from the United States and I have gotten in here at great risk so that I might talk to you."

"Talk," he said. "There is not much time. The guard goes by in another twenty minutes."

"Do you have a cellmate?" I asked.

"No."

"Then I will come in and talk," I said. I opened the door and stepped inside. I closed it and used the pick to lock it again. I had already decided that I would not try to go back out tonight. Getting out might be more dangerous than getting in, but there was another reason. Among the political prisoners there was a close bond; here, whatever bond there was would be a very loose one. There would certainly be some who would want to go out with me if they knew I was going. Refusal might bring some sort of outcry.

As I turned to face the blackness of the cell, I heard a faint pounding in the cell block and knew that other prisoners were being told that I had entered the cell in some way.

"How did you do that?" the old man's voice asked. It was coming from my right.

"I will tell you later," I said. "Is there another bed in here?"

"On the other side of the cell."

I groped my way to the left until my legs bumped into the bed. I sat down on it. "Does the guard make a close inspection?" I asked.

"No. Only to see that no one is up and doing anything."

"Good," I said. I felt around for the top of the blanket and then got in under it, pulling it up to my neck. "You shared a cell with Alberto de la Garra?"

"Yes."

"How did he die?"

"How do I know that I can talk to you?" the old man said.

"Rafael sent word to Manuel. What more do you want? They told you through the walls."

"You understood?" he asked. "You have been in prison?"

"Yes."

"In the United States?"

"There and in Spain and in Germany."

"Rafael was a good man," he said, "before he became mixed up with those politicians. He could scale a wall, that one. With the best."

"And you?" I asked.

"I am a burglar," he said. There was pride in his voice. "For forty years, Señor. The best in Puerto Torcido. Ask any of them. Most of them were taught by me."

"No me diga," I said. "You shared the cell with de la Garra. How did he die?"

"It was three o'clock in the morning," the old man said. "I have no watch, but I am a light sleeper. The guard had just made his twelfth trip. The door to the cell was unlocked and a man came in. As he turned I saw the outline of his face and I knew who he was. Then I shut my eyes and pretended to be asleep, for I knew what he would do. He put a flashlight on me. When he was satisfied I was asleep, he went over to the other who was sleeping heavily. He leaned over him, Señor, and he strangled him with his bare hands. There was much kicking and one or two groans and that was all, for he is a strong man. When he had finished he looked again to see that I was asleep. I tell you, I worked hard at it, for I did not want to die."

"Who did the killing?" I asked.

"Then," he said as though he hadn't heard me, "he took a sheet from the bed and tied one end of it around this de la Garra's neck. He stood on the bed and lifted the body up so that he could tie the sheet around the clothes hook on the wall. He looked at me again and left. The next morning the body was hanging there as though the man had done it himself. That morning they asked many questions, but I said that I had heard nothing during the night. Everyone else had slept soundly that night."

"Who was it?" I asked again.

"Carnicero," he said. "The Chief of Police."

Somehow, I wasn't surprised. Now that I knew, it didn't really do me any good, but I was still glad I had come. I knew that Moreno was dead and I knew that the killer of the American pilot had not committed suicide. No longer could I guess that the story about what had happened might be wrong.

"Listen to me, Pablo," I said. "I had a way of getting into the prison tonight. Through bribery. But I cannot get out the same way. I must wait here until morning and then claim that I was locked up during the night by mistake. Then I will get out. You and your comrades can say that you know nothing or that you heard someone being locked in during the night. Either story. But that is all. I know they are waiting to hear how I got in, so tell them all this."

He started pounding on the wall. I listened to it. He was telling them pretty much as I had said. We waited a long time while the message went from cell to cell. After a time, a short pounded message came back. I understood it, but said nothing.

"It is from Manuel," the old man said dryly. "He says that you must be a great fool to spend money to break into this prison. All of us got in without paying a single peso."

I laughed. "But tomorrow morning," I said, "I will walk out of here, *Dios mediante.*"

"Tomorrow we might all walk out, *Dios mediante.*"

"*Que Dios le oiga,*" I said. "Good night."

"*Que descanse usted bien,*" he said sarcastically.

It had been a tense night, so I fell asleep shortly after I pulled the blanket over my head. I slept through the night and only awakened in the morning to sounds of voices in the corridor. I looked around the cell. The old man was already sitting up on the bed, rolling himself a cigarette. He looked very much as I had imagined him from his voice. He was small and dark-skinned, his cheeks sunken, his hair white. The prison uniform hung loosely on his thin body.

"*Buenos dias,*" I said, swinging my feet off the bed and sitting up. "I seem to have come dressed wrong for this party."

He grinned at me. "Soon we will see," he said. "Everyone is waiting, and all along the block they are making bets. The man who walks out of Santa Monica by asking performs a greater miracle than the One who walked on water."

"Are you betting?" I asked. I got out a cigarette and lit it.

He nodded. "I have bet a sack of tobacco that you will walk out. Perhaps I am foolish, but I have never before seen a man walk through a cell door without keys, so I bet."

"What are the odds?" I asked.

"Two to one that you won't."

"If I were going to be around to collect, I'd bet myself," I said. "What's all the noise out there?"

"Breakfast."

"What do they serve?"

"Oatmeal. If one is lucky there will be only two or three worms in it."

"In that case," I said, "I don't think I'll wait for breakfast. I never like meat that early in the morning."

"We shall see," he said with the same grin.

Another minute and the breakfast detail showed up in front of the cell. It consisted of two guards, a wagon with a big can of oatmeal, and a stack of bowls and wooden spoons. One of the guards peered into the cell.

"Hola, anciano," he said. "Here is your—" He caught sight of me and his mouth dropped open. I think it was more the sight of a regular suit, white shirt, and necktie than just an extra man. *"Quién es?"* he demanded, pointing a finger at me.

The other guard crowded up to the cell door and stared at me. *"Quién es usted?"* he demanded.

"Send for the warden," I said. "I am a citizen of the United States and I demand to be released immediately. And you can be sure that the Benefactor will hear about this."

The second guard took one more look at me and turned and fled, muttering under his breath. The other stayed where he was, staring. Finally, he looked at the old man. "How did he get in here?" he asked. "Dressed like that!"

"Do I know what the police do?" the old man said. He was enjoying himself. "If they open the cell in the middle of the night and shove a man inside, do I get up and light a candle to see how he is dressed?"

The guard went back to staring at me, scratching his head.

In a few minutes there was the sound of hurrying footsteps along the corridor. The second guard came back. With him was another guard and a fat, perspiring man in a gray suit who had the harassed look of an official. "You see," the guard said. "There he is. I do not lie."

"Qué diablos," said the fat man. "But it is impossible. No one was brought in last night. There is no record. And the way he is dressed. It cannot be."

"Are you the warden?" I asked. "If so, I demand to be released at once."

"But you cannot be here," he said. "There is no record. How did you get here?"

"Some stupid policeman put me here," I said. "And for what? For drinking too much brandy. Turn me loose this minute or there will be the devil to pay."

"It is impossible," the warden said again.

"If you are not going to turn me loose," I said, "then I demand that you let me telephone. To the Palace."

"The Palace?" he said. He began to sweat more. "Who do you wish to phone at the Palace?"

"Raimundo Perrola. It will go hard with someone if you refuse."

The warden was a picture of indecision. He gnawed at his upper lip, and shifted his weight from one foot to another and back again. The very sound of "the Palace" frightened him, but slowly it began to dawn on him that it might also be his salvation. At least he would be spared further decisions. He recovered some of his dignity.

"Let him out," he said to the guard, "and take him to my office. Watch him closely. He may be dangerous." The guard unlocked the cell door and I stepped out. The guard relocked the door and turned to me, drawing his gun. "Move," he said sternly.

I waved to the old man. "Thank you for your hospitality," I said.

"De nada," the old man said with his grin. *"Aquí está usted como en casa."*

I marched down the corridor with the guard right behind me and the warden following at a safe distance. It made quite a procession. All along the cell block breakfast was forgotten as the prisoners watched. Most of them were grinning.

We went downstairs and to the office I had entered the night before. The warden went around and sat behind his desk. "Watch him carefully," he told the guard. "I myself will put through the call so that I know there is no trick." He picked up the phone and dialed a number.

Three times he asked for Perrola and announced he was the warden of the Fortress of Santa Monica. "Ah, Excellency," he said finally, and the tone of voice told me that Perrola must be on the phone. "This is the warden of the Fortress of Santa Monica. There is a man here who insists on speaking to your Excellency, and I put through the call to be sure there was no trick. ... His name? I do not know his name. Just a minute." He looked up at me. "Your name?"

"Milo March," I said.

He repeated it into the phone and a startled look came over his face. *"Espere un momento,"* he stammered. He held the phone out to me. I took it.

"Hello," I said.

"Ah, Mr. March," Perrola said. "What are you doing at

Santa Monica? Slumming?"

"Not quite," I said. "I'm afraid it's all pretty stupid. But I've called for one of those favors you offered. In this case, I will be even more grateful than Miss Mellany."

"What sort of favor?" he asked. His tone was just a little bit guarded.

"I'm afraid I got a little drunk last night," I said. "I'm not quite sure what happened. I think there may have been a fight of sorts. Anyway, a policeman brought me here and locked me up. The warden doesn't know whether to let me go or not. It seems they forgot to register me when I checked in."

"For being drunk?" he said. "The policeman must have been drunk, too. Well, I'll get right to work on it. Shouldn't take more than a few minutes. Put the warden back on, will you?" I knew why he was being so careful; he was afraid that Torcido might have ordered me arrested and he hadn't learned it yet. He'd check that first, then he'd get me out.

I handed the phone to the warden. He took it as if I were handing him a snake. He said "Yes, Excellency" six times and then hung up. He wiped the sweat from his face and stared at me unhappily. "We wait," he said.

So we waited. It was fifteen minutes before anything happened. Then somewhere outside, a door slammed. A moment later the door to the office burst open so violently that it cracked against the wall. Chief of Police Carnicero strode in. His gaze flicked over me and went directly to the warden.

"Pedazo de alcornoque," he snarled. "What is this thing?"

"I do not know," the warden stammered. "There is nothing

in the record. He says that he was drunk and some policeman brought him here and locked him up."

"On which side?"

"The criminal."

"Drunk," Carnicero snorted. "A policeman! *Es en cuento absurdo!* I will see about this. Let him go."

"Of course," the warden said. He looked at me. "You may go, Señor."

"Thank you," I said. I turned and walked past Carnicero, smiling at him.

"We will find out about this," Carnicero flung at the warden. Then I heard him walking out behind me.

We went out through the front door and then walked side by side. Nothing was said until we were out through the big iron gates where a police car and driver waited.

"I got in touch with your driver and told him to pick you up here," Carnicero said. "He should be here any minute."

"Le agradezco mucho su amabilidad," I told him.

"How did you get in there," he asked, "and why?"

"Too much to drink," I said vaguely. "And one of your policemen—"

"Absurdo," he snorted. "No policeman of mine would take you there even if you were dead drunk."

"Then perhaps it was someone disguised as a policeman," I said innocently.

"Señor," he said angrily, "you do not fool me for a minute. I am not fooled by the story about a manuscript by Christopher Columbus and I am not fooled by this story. I know what you are and what you are after. They have made me go carefully for the time being and they made me release you from here, but this will not last. They will soon see there is nothing to fear and they will listen to me."

"In that case," I said, "you'd better remember what I told you the day I arrived here."

He stared at me steadily, his eyes black with anger. "What was that?"

"That the next time you'd better shoot straighter—El Nariz—for I intend to."

"I will, Señor," he said softly. "Straighter and quicker." He turned and walked to the car, climbing into the back. The car leaped forward, the back tires spraying gravel.

NINE

The police car was barely out of sight when I heard another car approaching. I looked around. It was the Cadillac with Luis at the wheel. It braked to a stop in front of me. I opened the door and climbed in the front with him.

"Buenos días," I said cheerfully.

"Buenos días," he said, but he didn't sound cheerful. "I could have been here more quickly, but I saw the police car and thought it better to wait until he was gone. He did not sound in good humor when he told me to meet you here."

"He wasn't in good humor," I said. "He had to let me out of jail this morning, and it hurts him deeply to let any fish escape the net."

The Cadillac got under way. "You spent the night there?" Luis asked.

"Yes. It was very educational."

"You learned something?" he asked curiously.

I nodded. "Bernardo was right."

"About Moreno?"

"Yes. And I also learned how de la Garra died."

"How?"

"Under the thumbs of our friend Carnicero," I said. "Rather, I should say *your* friend. There was a little accident."

"Don Milo," Luis said, "I thought it was agreed that we

wouldn't talk about that."

"All right, Luis," I said. "Take me back to the hotel." I leaned back against the cushions and began to think ahead. I had an idea that Carnicero had been right about one thing: it probably wouldn't be long before Torcido might decide there was nothing to fear. I'd better move fast while he still believed part of my story.

When we reached the hotel, I told Luis to come up with me. Up in the room I gave him his fifty dollars, turned on the radio, poured a drink for each of us, and ordered some breakfast from room service. While I was waiting for the breakfast, I stripped and had a fast shower.

"That's the trouble with Santa Monica," I said as I came back into the room. "No showers, nothing to drink, and I understand the food is bad."

"True," Luis said, "but you must admit it is cheaper than here."

"Okay," I said. "Sit in the corner and be quiet for a while."

"*Es el colmo,*" he said, throwing his hands in the air.

"No," I said. "The last straw is when I stop paying you the twenty-five a day. Now shut up for a minute. Don't give me your lamentations. Just keep quiet." I sat down and ate my breakfast. It was ham and eggs, which was much better than oatmeal with only a few worms in it.

When I finished, I stretched out on the bed. "Sit there," I told him. "Cultivate your rear end as a means of earning money in this case. You think too much, *chico.*"

He sat in the corner, nursing his drink and sulking. It was all right with me; I ignored him. I relaxed and half slept and half thought. Sometimes I do my best thinking this way.

"Luis," I said sometime in the middle of this, "how many banks are there in Puerto Torcido?"

"Two," he said. "The Torcido National Bank and the Bank of the Americas. Why?"

"I like banks," I said. "They have money in them. You should like them too. … Where do the officials of the Monican Republic keep their money?"

"You make the joke," he said. "The Torcido National Bank is owned by the Benefactor. Where would you keep your money if you worked for him?"

"In my pocket," I said. "Okay. I get the point. Luis, you have a big family. Does one member of the family just happen to work for the Torcido National Bank?"

There was a moment of silence. "You are an evil man, Don Milo," he said. "You would not only corrupt me, you would corrupt my entire family. … My mother's aunt has a granddaughter who works in the bookkeeping department of the Torcido Bank. What do you want of her? Her virginity?"

"If she still has it, she's no relation of yours," I said. "I don't want much. Five weeks ago a man named Jaime Moreno vanished in New York City in the United States. You know of this?"

"I think I have heard of it," he said sarcastically.

"All I want," I said sleepily, "is to know what deposits were made since that time by Carnicero, Perrola, and Torcido. I will pay your mother's aunt's granddaughter a hundred dollars. I presume that you will collect a certain commission for arranging the matter."

He stared at me and got to his feet. "All right. I will see about it. I will be back within an hour or so."

"Luis," I said, "you are a gem beyond value. You know, it has just occurred to me that I might have saved myself a lot of trouble last night if I had thought to ask you if there are any of your relatives in Santa Monica. Are there?"

"My cousin Roberto," he said. "He made a small mistake."

I laughed. "Naturally. Large family, small mistakes, small accidents."

He gave me a reproachful look and went out. I didn't bother to turn the music down. I went back to sleep and didn't wake up until there was a knock on the door. I went and looked out. It was Luis. I opened the door and let him in. He'd been gone an hour and twenty minutes.

Luis nodded in answer to my look. "All three made deposits, Don Milo. Torcido deposited more than four hundred thousand pesos. That was just in his personal account. I did not get the deposits made for all his companies. *Caray!* Who could imagine that one could make so much money?"

"I doubt if he makes it," I said. "He just collects it. What about the others?"

"Carnicero put twenty thousand pesos in the bank and Perrola put in one hundred and thirty thousand. In American dollars."

"When?"

"The second day after Moreno disappeared in the United States," he said. Luis was no fool.

I whistled softly. I went over to my pants and got a hundred dollars and handed it to him. "I will add another hundred to it," I said, "if you can get me a photostat of the Perrola account showing that deposit."

"Is there to be no end?" he asked. *"Dios mío.* Each time you swallow something it only makes you hungrier. But I will try."

"I may even give you a bonus when I'm ready to leave," I said. "There are a few other things I'll want some help on, but I have every confidence that nothing is impossible for you."

He stared at me steadily. "What is it you want me to do now, Don Milo?" he asked. "Perhaps I should go hit Carnicero in his big nose? Or trample upon the feet of the Benefactor himself?"

"Nothing so difficult," I said. I grinned at him. "Tell me, do you have still another relative, one perhaps with a different last name and more distantly related, who might like a hundred dollars?"

"To do what?"

"You know the manuscript for which we have been looking? I think we will find it tomorrow morning."

"Qué pasa?"

"I have the manuscript," I explained. "All written by Christopher Columbus himself. Now I need some place to find it. So we need a relative who might have a few old things lying around."

He shrugged. "There is my mother's aunt. Her name is Emilia Ayala. She is old and has never thrown away anything. Will it make any difference that she submitted a list of her old things to you in the very beginning?"

I grinned at him. "You know, I wondered if some of those people who rushed to answer the ads weren't relatives of yours. No, it won't make any difference, Luis. We will find the manuscript at Aunt Emilia's, then, tomorrow morning. You'd better tell her. It might be embarrassing if she wasn't home. All right, that's one thing. Now, do you know of any sort of small building out of the city, but not too far, which is empty and can be rented? It should be someplace where there isn't too much traffic and not too near anyone's house."

"Why?" he asked.

"I've always wanted a little home away from home," I told him.

"It should be a place in which you can live?"

"No. I want it as more of a storage place."

"To store the manuscript, perhaps?" Luis asked sarcastically. "There is such a shack just north of the city. It has not been used for a long time."

"How big?"

"Six feet by eight feet. It has only the dirt floor, but it is in good condition otherwise."

"Can it be locked?"

"Yes. With the padlock."

"Which relative owns it?" I asked.

"A friend."

"You mean we're running out of relatives?" I said. "You disappoint me. All right, rent it for me."

"He will want ten dollars a month."

"Which means," I said with a grin, "that he'll rent it for about five dollars a month. Okay. I don't want it for more than a few days, but I'll give him fifty dollars. The rest is for keeping quiet. And be sure that you give him enough of the fifty so that he will keep quiet."

"Don Milo," he said in wounded tones, "you think I would steal from my friends?"

"Only if they weren't watching you," I said. "How are your connections with druggists, Luis?"

"You want to buy medicine?"

"It's medicine," I said. "Did you ever hear of Sodium Pentothal?"

He shook his head.

"Well, I want a hypodermic needle and enough Pentothal to keep a man unconscious for forty-eight hours. And tell the druggist not to forget the double-distilled water in which to dissolve it."

"Es el colmo," he said, throwing up his hands. "What do you take me for, Don Milo?"

"A rabbiter."

"Eh?"

" *'Dios confonda mensajero tan presto e tan ligero,' "* I said. "I thought you knew the poetry of Juan Ruiz."*

"You are trying to take advantage of me again," he said. "You know what a soft fellow I am at heart."

"Sure. As soft as steel."

"But Don Milo," he protested, "drugs and a hypodermic needle. And so that you can keep some man unconscious for forty-eight hours. What man? *Dios mío!* When I am finished with you, I will be in the Fortress of Santa Monica myself."

"Then I will use the beautiful steel picks which you helped

---

* "May God confound a messenger so prompt and so speedy." This line is from a poem about an archbishop who sends a messenger to woo a girl on his behalf, but instead the messenger wins her for himself. The next line says, "May God not reward a rabbit-hound [rabbiter] who retrieves game that way!"

me find to break in and bring you cigarettes," I said solemnly. "I put my fate in your hands, Luis. After all, are we not practically brothers? We almost died together on the mountain. Do we understand each other?" I went to my pants and got another hundred dollars. "We seem to have established a set price for everything, so here is a hundred dollars for the Pentothal and the hypodermic. I imagine that you will find a way to make a profit on it."

He took the hundred dollars and put it in his pocket. "I am beginning to lose my taste for money," he said. "Never have I seen such a madman as you. What good will money be if Carnicero gets around to considering me?"

"I'm sorry to spoil your simple pleasures," I said cheerfully, "but if all my ideas go through, you won't have to worry about Carnicero."

"Don't tell me," he said, clapping both hands over his ears. "My curiosity has been more than satisfied. I already know enough to make me an old man overnight. The brain staggers at the things you do, Don Milo."

"Without you and your relatives, I would be nothing," I said. "Now run along and do your errands."

He left. I made myself a drink and relaxed to think more about what I was going to do. I would need a lot of luck and would have to do a lot of ad-libbing, but I thought I had a chance to pull it off. I still had no idea how I would get Carnicero off alone, but I'd work out something. I was almost certain that Perrola would jump at the bait I was going to offer him; if he didn't, I'd have to take whatever profit I had and leave. In that case, I'd turn Carnicero over to the underground. The rest of it was going to be a matter of timing.

I went into the bathroom and shaved, then began to dress slowly. Now that action was about to start, I felt better than I had at any time since arriving in the Monican Republic.

Finally I phoned Juana, from a pay phone down in the lobby. "How are you, honey?" I said when she answered.

"I missed you last night," she said.

"I missed you, too, honey, but it couldn't be helped. I'll see you tonight, but I'll be a little late. I have to do something first. I'll probably reach your place about ten."

"Why so late?" she asked sulkily.

"Something I have to do."

"What?"

"Something," I said. "But don't worry. When I leave here, I'll have a nice little gun on me and I can take care of myself."

"I know you can," she said, "but I wish you'd tell me what you're going to do. Don't you trust me?"

"Sure, honey," I said. "I'll tell you all about it when I see you tonight. But this is big. It'll probably make or break the case, one way or the other. And somebody just might be listening. See you tonight." I hung up and went back upstairs.

Luis arrived about an hour later. He didn't look too happy about it, but he'd done fine. He did have a photostat of Perrola's bank sheet. I took it and taped it in under a dresser drawer. He also had the key to the shack north of the city. He gave it to me and also described exactly where it was and how to find it. I didn't expect to need it immediately, but I wanted to know. His mother's aunt would be home the following morning and would be very happy to sell me something that I already had. And he had the Pentothal and the hypodermic.

"The druggist says you must not give all of this to a man at once," he said. "It will kill him."

"I know," I said. I took it from him and put it in with my shirts, tucking it down inside of one shirt. "You did well, Luis. I trust that you made a reasonable profit for yourself on each one of the deals."

"Claro que sí," he said. "It is to be expected that I will be the wealthiest man in the Fortress of Santa Monica."

"Nonsense," I said. "They'll never put you in Santa Monica, Luis. If they did, you'd probably steal it, stone by stone." I looked at him. "Luis, my brother, is it that you are not feeling well? It seems to me that you are no longer your usual sunny self, running around reciting poetry until the very walls of Puerto Torcido ring with it."

"Who can recite poetry with a noose waving in his face?"

"You disappoint me, Luis," I told him. "François Villon and Christopher Marlowe both composed poetry with the noose staring them in the face. And there was an obscure poet who once composed a poem and recited it while the noose was placed around his neck. He hadn't quite finished it when they dropped him. Of course, he wasn't a very good poet, which may be why they hanged him."

"Do not jest about such things, Don Milo," he said. "When do you think you will return to the United States?"

"Such haste to get rid of me is unseemly. But I expect I'll go soon. And then you can return to your carefree life of little thievery, little accidents—and little money. In a few months, you'll probably be bragging that you did everything yourself and the *norteamericano* did nothing."

"I will not even whisper to myself that I knew you, Don Milo. I will say to myself that it was only a bad dream which it is better to forget. That is, if, *Dios mediante,* Carnicero doesn't leap upon me the minute you are gone, thinking that it is better to grab a pebble than to let the entire mountain escape."

"I don't think Carnicero will bother you," I told him. "All right, Luis. I guess you can quit for the day. If I need you later, I'll get in touch with you at the number you gave me."

"Está bien," he said, and left.

I called downstairs for the newspapers and some more ice. When they came I had another drink and read the papers until it was time to go meet Elena. I gave myself a few extra minutes. I put my gun and holster away in the drawer and went downstairs. Out on the street, I looked for a taxi.

"Señor March," a voice said.

I recognized the voice and I wasn't surprised to hear it. I turned and looked at Carnicero. He was sitting in a police car parked at the curb. There was another policeman with him. Carnicero got out of the car. There was a hopeful look on his face.

"One moment, Señor March," he said. He waited until I walked over to him. "Where are you going?"

"I have a date," I said. "With a very beautiful woman. I will buy her a drink and perhaps even take her to dinner. When I leave her, I have a date with another beautiful woman. I find the Monican women so interesting they are about to take up all of my time."

"A su abuela con esta historia," he said—a suggestion that I should go tell that story to my grandmother. "Do you have any objection to being searched?"

"Of course I do," I said. "Will it do me any good?"

"None at all," he said with a tight smile. "Pedro, watch him." I noticed then that the other policeman in the car was holding a gun in his lap.

I held my hands away from my body and Carnicero swiftly patted my clothes. A baffled look came to his face. He repeated the search, this time feeling across my chest and over my pockets very carefully.

"One search is properly legal," I told him, "but the second time, one begins to suspect that too much familiarity is being tried."

He stepped back, his face dark with anger. "Señor, if you are trying to play games with me ..."

"I?" I said in surprise. "This little game was all your idea. When a man is going to hold a beautiful woman in his arms, it is not polite to wear a gun. But you wouldn't know about those things. One does not expect it of a *chulo*."

For a minute I thought he would not be able to contain his anger. I could see him clenching his fists at his sides. "Señor," he said, his voice hoarse with effort, "one day you will go too far. Since you have no gun on you, perhaps I should search your room again."

"Why not?" I said lightly. "Be my guest. Here's the key. You may leave it with the desk clerk when you're finished. In the meantime, I'm late for my date."

He stared at me for a minute, while I hoped it would work. I hadn't counted on him wanting to search the room again.

"I do not need your key," he said arrogantly. "But I will search it sometime when you are less prepared for it than you obviously are now. And Señor ..."

"Yes?"

"Remember what I told you this morning. At the moment, my orders are not to do anything to you unless I catch you in an illegal act. But this will not last. Soon it will change—perhaps today, perhaps tomorrow. When it does"—he grinned without humor—*"cuidado."*

"I'm always careful," I answered. "Good night—El Nariz."

"Hasta luego," he said.

I turned and walked down the street a few feet, then stopped to hail a taxi. I had him take me to the café. The bartender greeted me like an old friend and waved me on to the back. She was there in the same booth.

"Why don't you sit somewhere else just to surprise me?" I said. "I'm beginning to think that you sleep here, too."

She gave me a wan smile. "Did you see my brother?"

"I saw him," I said. "I gave him your message. He was pleased to get it. He said everything was well, even though confining. He doesn't want to escape. He expects them to let him out shortly after I leave."

"When do you expect to leave?" she asked.

I threw up my hands. "I'm beginning to think that no one here likes me. Everyone wants to know when I'm leaving. You get the same answer. When I'm finished with my work here."

"How did you get to see him?" she asked. "They gave permission?"

"I didn't ask for it. I walked in and they let me out this

morning because they didn't have any record of me being put in."

The bartender arrived with our drinks. He was obviously very proud of himself for not having to be told what to bring. We waited until he had left.

"I do not understand," she said.

"It's better if you don't," I told her. "Look, Elena, I'm going to go stir crazy if I have to stay in this booth. Will you go somewhere and have dinner with me?"

She hesitated a minute, then nodded.

"How are you coming with your work?" she asked. "Have you learned anything about Dr. Moreno?"

"Still wanting to know how soon I'll leave?" I said. "I've picked up a few things. Dr. Moreno is dead, if you really want to know."

She stared at me. "You are sure?"

"Positive."

"Then your work is finished, is it not?"

"No," I said. "It's only begun. Finish your drink and let's go to dinner."

We drank and left the booth. I paid the bartender and we went out on the street and found a taxi. I let her suggest a place to have dinner and then told the driver to take us there. I leaned back in the seat and put my arm around her. She glanced at me out of the corners of her eyes. I pulled her to me. For just a minute her lips answered mine, then she pushed herself away. Her fingers left a stinging trail across my cheek.

"Señor March," she said, "not all Monican girls are like Juana Ramos."

"So it would seem," I admitted. "Still, there's only one way to find out. You have a very sweet mouth, Elena."

"Thank you—but it is not for the plucking by anyone who comes along."

"I got the point the first time you hit me," I said dryly. "By the way, you were right about your friend Juana."

"What do you mean?"

"She works for Carnicero."

"How do you know?"

"I set a little trap for her today," I said. "And Carnicero showed up. That may not prove it for your people, but it proves it to me."

"I knew it," she exclaimed. "What are you going to do about it?"

"I'm going to see her later," I said.

"She probably won't object if you use the approach you just tried on me," she said slyly.

I grinned down at her. "Probably not. And you're just like her. You want to know too many answers. Why can't you be satisfied just to sit there and be pretty instead of trying to make like a spy or running around trying to shoot people?"

"I told you I was sorry about that," she said stiffly.

"So you did. Well, now we're even. You're sorry you tried to shoot me and I'm sorry I tried to kiss you. Only I'm not. The sample was pretty nice."

"Men are all alike," she said scornfully.

"Sure. And women are different. It's a great difference. You ought to let me explain it to you sometime."

The taxi stopped in front of the restaurant before she could think of an answer. I paid the driver and we went inside. She had another vermouth while I had two martinis. Then we had dinner. It was a pretty good imitation of a Spanish dinner. She was very intense and kept trying to talk about the underground and what was happening in the Monican Republic, but I finally got her to talking about her schoolwork and then she relaxed a little.

I dragged dinner out as long as I could, but finally it was close to ten o'clock and I knew I'd better get on the move. "Okay," I said, "it's been fun in spite of the right hook to the jaw. Now I will take you home and go on my merry way."

"I can get home alone," she said.

"Sure you can. You're a big girl now. In fact, that's why I want to take you home." I paid the bill and we left the restaurant. We were barely out of the restaurant when our way was barred. I looked up. It was Carnicero.

"Oh, no," I said. "Not again in the same night. Well, go ahead." I started to lift my arms.

"No, Señor," he said. "I do not wish to search you. My only word for you now is that you should be more careful with whom you associate. Your companion is part of a group which is the enemy of the state. Communists. Her brother is already in prison."

"Thanks for the warning," I said. "Now, if you'll excuse us, I have to get her home before she's exposed to worse influences."

"You do not understand," he said. "Señorita Sanjurjo is being arrested."

"You can't do that," I said.

"Stay out of it," she whispered.

"Can't I?" he asked. There was something close to joy on his face. "Are you intending to stop me, Señor?"

"No," I said, knowing it was what I had to say. "Don't worry, Elena. I will do something to get you out."

"There is nothing you can do," she said. "And I have been expecting it."

"Come, Señorita," Carnicero said. He took her by the arm and led her to the police car parked at the curb. He helped her politely into the rear seat of the car and climbed in after her. He closed the door and looked through the window to make sure that I was watching. Then he lifted one hand and deliberately smashed her across the mouth.

I had already taken two steps toward the car before I realized that this was the one thing I must not do. It was exactly what Carnicero wanted, and it wouldn't help either one of us. I stopped and shoved my hands in my pockets so he wouldn't see the clenched fists. He grinned wolfishly at me through the window, then the police car drove away.

I stood there long enough to get better control of myself, then finally hailed a taxi. I had the driver take me back to the hotel and wait. I went upstairs and took the holster and gun from beneath my shirts and buckled it around my chest. I went back down to the cab and gave the driver Juana's address.

It was a few minutes past ten when the cab stopped in front of her apartment house. I paid off the driver and went up. Her apartment was on the second floor. I knocked on the door.

"Come in," she called through the door.

I opened it and walked in. She was standing in front of a full-length mirror admiring herself. She looked up and smiled at me. "You are late," she said.

"Yeah," I said. "I'm late. But I might not have been here at all."

"What do you mean?"

"Tell me, *cariño*," I said, "how much does Carnicero pay you?"

"I do not know what you mean," she said.

"How much did Carnicero pay you for telling him I was going to be carrying a gun when I left the hotel today? The gun he couldn't find. This one." I slipped the gun from my holster and held it loosely in my hand.

Her eyes got big as she looked at it. "What are you going to do?" she asked.

"Did I look like I was going to do something?" I asked. I put the gun back in the holster. "How much does he pay you?"

"I do not work for him."

"Oh, no? Baby, you were the only person I told that I was going out on something and that I would be carrying a gun. And I didn't make the call from my room; I'm sure they listen in on that phone. And Carnicero was waiting for me when I got downstairs. He knew what he expected to find and was surprised when he didn't find it. You were the only one who could have sent him on that little errand."

"No," she said.

"Come here," I said. I reached for her and she started to spin away. I tried to grab her shoulder, but instead I got a handful of dress. And she was on the move. There was a ripping sound and the dress came away in my hand. She was left in just a wisp of silk around her middle. Automatically, her arms went up to cover her bare breasts.

"Why bother?" I asked her. "I've seen them before. The tools of your trade. How does it feel, *cariño,* to go to bed with a man and then telephone a report on him to someone who wants to kill him? Does it make going to bed more exciting?"

"Please ..."

"Does it?"

When the dress ripped from her body, all the fight seemed to go out of her. "I am sorry, Milo," she said faintly. "I really liked being with you. I didn't want to report on you. But I had to. Carnicero made me do it. And he has never paid me anything."

"No? For what, then? Love of Torcido?"

"No. My father is in Santa Monica. It is only because of the work I have done for Carnicero that he is still alive. If I refused, they would kill him."

"You're a bigger fool than if you'd done it for money," I said. "You haven't really kept your father alive. The minute you're no longer useful, they'll kill him—and probably you, too. And that minute is practically on top of you, baby. I don't even have to tell the underground about you; they're already certain. You'd better start picking a soft place to land."

"What are you going to do?" she asked again.

"Nothing. Just get out in the clean air." I tossed the dress to her. "Good night, baby. It's been nice." I turned and walked out through the door without looking back.

As I reached the street, a car screeched to a stop in front of the building. The door opened and Carnicero got out. He was alone. Except for a gun in his hand.

"Señor," he said, "what a pleasure to run into you again. Please get your hands above your head. Quickly. I think I will try searching you again."

TEN

Raising my hands, I cursed softly to myself. I didn't have to have a diagram drawn for me. I'd been foolish just because I wanted to tell Juana off. I hadn't stopped to think. Since Juana was spying for them, they probably had her apartment bugged. Carnicero had known I was going there and was smart enough to guess that I might know it was Juana who had tipped him off for the first search. So he'd alerted his man who listened, who in turn had probably reached him by radio.

"Don't you ever get tired of this?" I asked.

"No," he said. "I never tire of my work. Be careful, Señor. Do not make any sudden moves."

He stepped around behind me, holding his gun against my back, and patted me under the left arm. He grunted with satisfaction and reached in to snake my gun from its holster.

"This is most serious, Señor," he said. "Carrying a gun in my country is expressly forbidden. It is a most serious offense."

"I'll bet it is," I said. "Especially if it's somebody you want to get. But even with that as an excuse, I don't think they'll like it if you kill me."

"It all depends," he said. "Were you to try to run or to take my gun away from me, I would have no choice but to shoot you. They would understand that. But I do not intend to kill you—just yet."

"Sweet of you," I murmured.

"I think," he said, "we will go upstairs and visit with Juana."

"What? No jail?"

"Not just yet. I wish to have a private talk with you and then we will see what is to happen. Upstairs, Señor." I turned and walked back upstairs, wondering what the pitch was. When we reached Juana's door I stopped. "Open the door and walk in," he ordered.

I threw open the door and went in with Carnicero right behind me. Juana had already put on a robe and was just coming out of the bedroom. Her face stiffened with fear as she saw the two of us.

"Ah, now we are just three friends together," Carnicero said. Then he confirmed the guess I had made downstairs. "You may now go home, Arturo," he said loudly. "It will not be necessary to listen anymore tonight."

"You're signing the station off early," I said. "The main event is just about to start."

"For you, yes," he said. "Go sit in that chair." He jabbed me in the kidneys with the gun and I went across the room and sat in the chair. Then I got my first look at the gun he was holding. It was a .32 and it looked like an American make. It was probably the same gun he'd been carrying in New York.

"What's happening?" Juana asked. Her voice quavered.

"Be quiet," Carnicero said. "What happens does not concern you. I merely want to use your apartment for a few minutes. Now, then, Señor, there are some things I would know from you." He came over to stand in front of me. "With whom have you been conspiring in my country?"

"Well, there's Juana and you "

He swung his arm and the barrel of the gun slashed across the side of my face. It was hard enough to jar me. I felt a warm trickle on my cheek and knew he'd drawn blood.

"With whom?" he repeated. "For example, who helped you to get into the prison last night?"

"Largase, hombre," I told him. "Buzz off, man."

He hit me on the other side of the face, a flat blow with the gun that made the room spin. When I got my eyes back in focus, he was grinning at me. "I am being polite," he said, "but if you persist in this stubbornness, perhaps I will get rough."

"I'm sure you're quite capable of it—El Nariz," I said.

"You will tell me what I want to know," he said with satisfaction. He licked his lips as though in anticipation.

"You—you are El Nariz?" Juana asked suddenly. Her voice was shrill.

"He's El Nariz, honey," I said.

Then she was at Carnicero's side, clawing at his arm. Not fighting, but more as if she had to get his attention. "But it was El Nariz who killed my brother," she said. "He lived long enough to say the name. And you told me that you would find him. That was the night I—I—"

Carnicero shifted the gun to his left hand, then he half turned and smashed her across the face with the flat of his hand. I didn't wait to see what happened to her. The minute he started to move, I was out of the chair. He saw me coming and he turned back fast. But not fast enough. My fist caught him on the jaw, spinning him back the other way and sending him staggering across the room. I went after him.

He bumped against the wall and straightened up. He tried to swing the gun around. I chopped down with the edge of my hand and the gun slipped from his fingers. He started to reach for his pocket where he'd put my gun. I drove a left hook into his belly, then crossed a right to his mouth. There was a pulpy sound as my fist hit his lips. He forgot about the gun and started to bring his hand up to protect his face. But he was too late with that too. The second punch had set him up. I swung my right again and this time I put all my weight behind it. I knew it was good when I could feel the blow all the way along my arm. His head snapped back and cracked against the wall.

All the expression faded from his face as though it had been wiped off. His knees bent and he slowly slid down the wall to the floor. I bent over and took my gun from his pocket. I walked over and picked the other one up from where it had fallen. Then I looked around for Juana. She was sitting on the floor, blood and tears running down her face. The blood was from her nose, so it wasn't serious.

I went over and sat down in the chair. I felt my own face. It was bleeding, but not badly. But it was going to be pretty sore for several days.

"He—he was the one who killed my brother," Juana said. She sounded as if she were talking in her sleep.

"He's killed all sorts of brothers and sisters," I said. "He's a nice little playmate. Now, get up and go put cold water on your face. It'll stop the bleeding."

She got up and went obediently into the bathroom. I sat and watched Carnicero. In one way I had him right where I wanted him, except that it was too early. It began to look as if I were going to do my Christmas shopping early.

My face and head hurt. "Juana," I called, "got anything to drink in the house?"

"A bottle of brandy," she said dully.

"Bring it to me."

She came in a minute with it. I took the cork out and tilted the bottle to my mouth. Maybe it didn't do any good, but it made me think I felt better.

Carnicero groaned and began to come around. Finally he propped himself up on one elbow and looked around. His gaze finally reached me and stopped.

"Nice, huh?" I said. "That ought to teach you not to hit women." I stood up and moved away from the chair. "Now it's your turn to sit in the chair. Get moving, *chulo*."

He got up slowly and went over to the chair without once taking his gaze from me.

"Juana, you stand over there where I can see you without straining myself," I said. I walked over to Carnicero. "Now, *chico,* let's look at my situation. You have made it most embarrassing for me. I don't dare let you go; in fact, things would be no worse for me if I were to kill you. You understand this?"

He stared at me silently.

"In the meantime," I said, "I think I will teach you the proper way to do what you were trying to do a while ago."

I reached out and smashed the barrel of my gun across his nose. I could hear the bone break as it landed. "You see," I said, "you jumped around too much. It does a lot more good to work on one spot. Like this." I hit him again on the nose. This time a strangled sob escaped from his lips. The blood spurted out over his shirt.

"And there mustn't be too much time in between blows," I said. I brought the gun down again. This time he fainted.

"Dios mío," I heard the girl whisper.

I waited. In a couple of minutes, he opened his eyes and his face once more contorted with pain. I reached out and slashed with the gun barrel again.

"No más," he groaned. *"Dios mío.* What do you want?"

"Use the phone," I said. "Call wherever you have to and give orders for Elena Sanjurjo to be released at once."

He hesitated. I hit him again across the nose. Not as hard as before, but hard enough. The groan rattled in his throat.

"Pick up the phone," I said.

He reached out and took the phone. He started dialing, having trouble getting the numbers because of the tears in his eyes.

"And don't try anything," I said. "One wrong word and I'll kill you and take my chances on getting away."

He nodded and finished dialing. "Carnicero here," he said a moment later. "Turn the Sanjurjo girl loose. ... *Pedazo de alcornoque!* Turn her loose. Now."

He replaced the phone and looked at me. His nose was already beginning to puff up. "I think," he said hoarsely, "I will kill you very slowly for this, Señor."

"I haven't finished with you yet," I told him. I reached out and hit him across the point of the jaw with the gun barrel. He slumped forward, out. That boy had a glass jaw.

"Go put a dress on," I told Juana.

"Why?"

"Because I told you to. Get going."

She went into the bedroom. I took another drink from the bottle of brandy and followed her into the bedroom. She was just starting to put the dress on, but I paid no attention to her. I stripped the two sheets from the bed and went back into the living room. I waited until she came in.

"What are you going to do with me?" she asked.

"Nothing," I said. "You're going to help me."

"No," she said.

"You want him found in your apartment?" I asked.

She paled. "I will help you. What do you want me to do?"

"Carry these," I said, tossing her the sheets, "and come on." I got Carnicero up and pulled one of his arms around my neck. With one arm around him I could carry him, and if we ran into anyone on the stairs, it might just look as if I were helping a drunk along.

We went down the stairs that way. I sent Juana ahead to see if there was anyone on the street. There wasn't. I had her open the back door of the police car and I carried Carnicero over and put him in.

"Now you get in and drive," I told her.

She hesitated, but finally got in behind the wheel. I knew she was afraid to drive the car, but more afraid not to. I climbed in the back where I could watch Carnicero.

"Drive up north of the city," I said. "You'd better go by back streets as much as possible until we're out of the city."

She nodded and started the car. She made a U-turn and went down a little side street. We rode silently for the ten or fifteen minutes it took us to get out of the city. Then I gave her the directions as Luis had given them to me. I was relieved when the headlights showed a tiny shack just where he'd said it would be. I hadn't intended using it so quickly, but I was glad I had it.

I unlocked the door and carried Carnicero inside. He was still unconscious. I tore up the two sheets and tied him securely. Then I used another strip to gag him. When I was sure there was no chance of his getting free, I slipped his own gun in his pocket and went back to the car.

"Drive to the airport," I told her, getting in front beside her.

"Are you leaving?" she asked.

"No, I'm not leaving," I said. I realized that she was shivering. It wasn't cold, so it must have been fear.

It took us another ten minutes to reach the airport. I had her park the car some distance from the terminal.

Then we got out and walked over. I glanced at the board. There was a plane leaving for Miami in twenty minutes. I left Juana standing and went over and bought a ticket. I went back and gave it to her.

"Get on that plane," I said. "It takes off in twenty minutes."

She looked at the ticket and back to me. "But—but my clothes ..."

"You want clothes or you want to live?" I asked.

She shivered again. "I'll go."

"Now, look," I said. "When you land in Miami, you'll be arrested because you don't have the proper papers. I can't do anything tonight, but I'll get on the phone the first thing in the morning and get someone to try to help you. Maybe it can be arranged for you to stay there. But after that you'll be on your own."

"Thank you," she said.

I stayed and watched her climb the stairs and disappear into the plane. She was no good any way you looked at it, but I felt sorry for her. Besides, it wasn't going to be safe for me if she stayed in Puerto Torcido.

I waited until I saw the plane take off. Then I went back and found a phone booth. I dialed the number that Luis had given me. On the tenth ring he answered, his voice heavy with sleep.

"Pick me up at the airport as quickly as you can," I told him.

"But Don Milo—" he began.

"Pick me up first and argue about it later," I interrupted. "Make it fast." I hung up.

I went back to the counter and asked about the next plane to New York City. There was one at six in the morning that would get there at three in the afternoon. I made a reservation in the name of E. Sanjurjo and paid for the ticket. I was beginning to feel as if I were supporting half the population of the Monican Republic.

I sat down on one of the benches and waited. It was another twenty minutes before Luis arrived, still rubbing the sleep from his eyes. But he came fully awake the minute he saw my face.

"What happened, Don Milo?" he asked.

"Cut myself shaving," I said. "Let's go."

We went out to the car and got in.

"It is late," he said. "Where do you wish to go?"

"To your house," I said. "Then you can go back to sleep and I will take the car."

"Ca!" he said. "That would not do, Don Milo. Suppose they should find out?"

"Well, take your pick," I said. "You can drive me if you ask no questions and are willing to maybe be more involved. Otherwise, give me the car."

He sighed. "I will drive you. It will make me nervous, but not so nervous as not knowing what is happening with the car. Where to, Don Milo?"

"The hotel first," I said.

When we reached the hotel, I went upstairs while Luis waited. I got out an ampule of Pentothal and dissolved it in the distilled water. Then I filled the hypodermic, wrapped it in a handkerchief, and put it in my pocket. I went back downstairs.

"To the shack," I told Luis.

"Dios mío," he muttered, but he drove off without asking any questions.

Again I had him wait in the car when we reached the shack. I unlocked the door and went in. Carnicero was conscious. I could hear him thrashing around. I crouched down beside him and used my knife to cut the coat and shirtsleeves. I got out the hypodermic and struck a match so I could see a vein. I pushed the needle in and pressed on the plunger. I could see Carnicero's eyes bulging with fear.

"Cálmese," I told him. "This is just something to make you sleep well. Happy dreams."

When the hypodermic was empty, I wrapped it up again and put it back in my pocket. I went out and locked the door. I climbed in beside Luis. 'Now to the Café Bendito," I said.

He started the car without a word and drove back into the city. He soon pulled up in front of the café. I told him to wait again and I went in. The bartender was just getting ready to close. He smiled at the sight of me.

"You know the young lady I've been meeting in here?" I asked.

He nodded. "I know her and her family for many years."

"Where does she live?"

The smile vanished from his face. "Señor," he said sternly, "it is already past three o'clock in the morning. The señorita lives alone and it is not right—"

"Look," I interrupted, "I'm not in a very good mood. I've been beaten up and I'll be lucky if that's all that happens to me. I'm not going to rape her; I want to save her from more trouble. Now, do you tell me where she lives or do I have to come over the bar and beat it out of you?"

He looked at me and his mustache quivered. "Señor—" he began.

I took my gun out and held it in my hand. "Where does she live?"

He gulped. "In—in her brother's house on the Avenida Quixote."

"Thanks," I said. "What number?"

"Forty-three."

I put the gun away and went back to the car. "To forty-three Avenida Quixote," I said, getting in.

He started the car. "That is where the prisoner Felipe Sanjurjo lived," he said.

"Brilliant of you," I said.

"You are going to see the sister," he announced.

"Sure," I snapped. "I'm going to sing a love song under her window. Isn't that what one is supposed to do with Spanish girls?"

"Not at three in the morning," he said. "If we are seen there, it will go bad with you. And bad with me if I haven't reported it."

I laughed. "You tell Carnicero tomorrow," I said. "I don't mind at all. But be sure you tell only him."

He looked at me curiously but said nothing. In a few more minutes we stopped in front of a small house. It was completely dark.

"Wait," I said. I got out and went to the front door of the house. I knocked on the door. There was no answer.

I knocked louder and kept it up. After a while there was a faint sound from inside.

"Who is there?" she asked. She sounded frightened.

"Milo March," I said.

"What do you want?" she asked. "It is very late. I was only released from the prison a couple of hours ago."

"I know," I said. "I arranged it. Now get dressed and pack your suitcase and come on."

"But why?" she asked. "I do not understand."

"Dios confonda," I said. "Nobody in this place ever understands anything.

Everything is questions. Why? What? Where? Just get dressed and packed and get out here. I'll wait, but not too long for then I'll come in and dress you and carry you out."

I heard her gasp. Then she said, "Wait for me."

I went back to the car and sat down. I lit a cigarette and Luis and I waited in silence. I don't know how long it was, but I was on my third cigarette and getting impatient when she finally appeared, suitcase in hand. I got out and took the suitcase from her. We both got in the back seat.

"Back to the airport," I told Luis.

"What is this about?" she asked as Luis swung the car around.

"You," I said, "are taking a six o'clock plane back to New York City. The reservation is already made and the ticket is paid for."

"I will not," she said. "There are things for me to do here."

"Sure, like rotting in jail, which is what you would be doing if it hadn't been for me," I said. "Look, honey, there's a very good chance that all hell is going to start popping around here in the next day or two. And you'll be right in the middle of it if you're here. So you're getting on the plane even if I have to knock you out and carry you aboard."

"Well!" she exclaimed. Just then we passed a streetlight and she must have gotten her first look at my face. "What happened to your face?" she asked.

"I ran into an argument," I said. "Baby, this isn't a game. It's for keeps. I'm stirring up a lot of things. You might get blamed for some of them. And so will your brother if you are. You leave, and you and your brother will be safer."

"My brother?" she said. I could hear her weakening. "Well, all right. What are you doing?"

"What I came down here to do," I said wearily. "I never saw so many people who wanted to know my business."

She could sulk just as easily as Luis. After that she sat over in the corner of the car and kept quiet. There was still a lot of time to kill when we got to the airport, so I took her in for coffee. We had three or four cups of it. I stayed with her until it was time to board the plane. Then I waited until they rolled the stairs away.

"Now we go to the hotel," I told Luis when I had awakened him in the car.

We drove straight back to the hotel. I told Luis to come up with me. When we got upstairs I got the operator on the phone and told her I wanted to be called at eight.

"You can take one bed and I'll take the other," I told Luis. "We start again at eight in the morning, so there's no point in your going home."

He groaned. "Are all *norteamericanos* like you?" he asked. "If so, I do not think I will go there. It would be impossible to write poetry in such a climate."

"Go to sleep," I told him. I stripped off my own clothes and tumbled into the bed. I was asleep almost as soon as my head hit the pillow.

And it seemed to me that I was barely asleep when I was awakened by the ringing of the phone. I fumbled for the receiver and finally found it.

"*Buenos días, señor,*" the operator said. "You wished to be called at eight o'clock."

"Yeah, but not so cheerfully," I said. "Give me room service." When I got them I ordered two big pots of coffee and two orders of ham and eggs. I asked them to bring a bottle of water, too. Then I went in and had a shower. That made me feel a little better. I looked in the mirror. My face had looked worse. The cuts weren't bad. Both cheeks were various shades of green and blue, and I had one black eye. Otherwise, I looked fine.

I went back into the other room and had a small shot of Canadian Club without ice. By then I was fully awake. I went over and shook Luis awake.

"Dios," he said. He regarded me malevolently from one eye. "What is it that you have against the sleep?"

"Nothing," I said cheerfully. "But we have a lot of things to do today." I splashed some Canadian Club into a glass and handed it to him. "Here. Have an eye opener." I don't think he realized what it was I was giving him, but he immediately drank it all down like it was orange juice. Then both eyes popped open and he came out of bed, swearing.

"You are ruining me for life, Don Milo," he said. "Until you came along, I was a happy and secure man. Now look at me."

"That's what happens when you start getting rich," I told him. "Run along and wash the sleep out of your eyes. Breakfast is on its way up."

The breakfasts arrived just as he returned from the bathroom. It made both of us feel better. Even Luis began looking more cheerful after his third cup of coffee. But he changed quickly when he saw me start to fill the hypodermic. When it was full, I wrapped it in the handkerchief and put it back in my pocket. Then I took the drawer out of the dresser and removed the Spanish manuscript I had taped there the day I arrived. I wrapped it in a newspaper.

Finally, I put the bottle of water in my pocket. "Come on," I said. *"Nos vamos ahora."*

We went down and got into the car. "There is no need to tell me," Luis said. "We drive first to the shack."

"Right."

"Dare I ask who you have there?" he asked.

"Better not. It's much better if you know nothing."

"Que Dios le oiga," he said earnestly.

We drove up north of the city and stopped at the shack. I went in and got a drowsy Carnicero to sip some water before giving him another shot. I had thought about trying to feed him but gave it up. It wouldn't hurt him to go a couple of days without food. I went back to the car and I told Luis to take me to his mother's aunt from whom I was going to buy the manuscript.

She lived in a small shack on the other side of the city. She was a tiny little woman with a wrinkled, merry face and I liked her at once. We talked generally for a few minutes. Then I gave her the money and I unwrapped the manuscript and showed her what it was she was selling. Then Luis and I went back to the hotel. I walked through the lobby, holding the manuscript and grinning broadly.

When I got upstairs, I put in a call to the Palace. I went through the usual run of voices until I finally got the last secretary. I told him that it was very important for me to speak to the Generalissimo himself if it was at all possible. He said he'd see.

"*Buenos días,* Señor March," another voice finally said. It was the dictator himself. "What can I do for you?"

"I just wanted to tell you," I said, "that my mission has been successful."

There was a moment of silence while he digested that. He hadn't really believed in my manuscript, and now I was saying I had it.

"It has?" he said finally. "My congratulations."

"I am thinking of returning to New York tomorrow," I said, "and I wondered if I could make an appointment for tomorrow morning. I would like to show you the manuscript before I leave with it, and of course I'd like to see your private museum which you offered to show me."

"Of course," he said. "Come in at ten, Señor March."

"Thank you, Generalissimo," I said. I hung up and grinned to myself. Next I called the airport and made a reservation for noon the following day just in case anyone checked up on me. Then I called the Palace again and asked for Raimundo Perrola. I got him much quicker.

"How are you, Mr. March?" he asked. "And how is your lovely employer?"

"Fine," I said. "I wonder if I could run over and see you for a few minutes."

"Certainly," he said. "Come right away, if you like."

I went down and had Luis drive me to the Palace. I told him to wait. I went inside and was shown in to Perrola almost immediately.

"It's good to see you again," he said, giving me another one of those manly handshakes. "How are you progressing?"

"Wonderful," I said, trying to look like a happy man. "I've found the manuscript."

"The Columbus manuscript?" he asked. He looked as startled as he sounded. He also had not believed in it. "I am delighted. Where did you find it?"

"Some little old woman who lives on the edge of the city. She had it in with a lot of junk in an old trunk. She doesn't even know where it came from, but thinks everything in the trunk had belonged to her grandmother. Of course, it'll have to be examined by experts, but I think it's authentic. And in good condition."

"Excellent," he said. "Miss Mellany will be delighted. Have you told her yet?"

"No. That is one of the reasons I wanted to see you."

"So?"

"I know that she will be grateful for all the help you've given me," I said. "And something occurred to me. You mentioned that you are in New York quite often. Do you expect to be there this coming weekend, or in the near future?"

"I might be," he said. He looked like a small boy who sensed candy in the offing. "Why?"

"Well, I'm going back tomorrow. I'm sure Miss Mellany will want to celebrate finding the manuscript, and I thought if you were going to be there, I'd suggest that she invite you out so that she can thank you in person."

"I would like to meet her," he said. He drummed on the desk with his fingers. "I don't see any reason why I shouldn't be there even this weekend."

"Fine. I'll call her then as soon as I get back to the hotel."

"Why not call her from here?" he suggested.

"You're sure it won't be an imposition?"

"Not at all." He pushed one of the telephones toward me.

Hoping that Merry remembered what I had told her about taking her cues from me, I picked up the receiver and put through the call to Westport, Connecticut. The operator said that she would ring back as soon as she had the party, and I hung up.

"The operator will call as soon as it's through," I explained.

"Excellent," he said. "By the way, what happened to your face?"

"I'm not sure," I said. "I guess it happened the other night when I ended up in that jail of yours. I told you I thought there was a fight of some sort."

He laughed. "That was quite an experience. The poor Chief of Police is still going crazy trying to find out what happened. But naturally the policeman who made a mistake like that isn't going to come forward and admit it."

The phone rang. I picked it up and answered. "Here is your party," the operator said.

"Hello, Milo," Merry said sleepily. "What's the idea of calling me up at this horrible hour?"

"I've found the Columbus manuscript," I said trying to sound excited.

There was a moment of silence. She probably had to stop and figure out what the Columbus manuscript was. "Oh, that's wonderful," she said finally.

"Isn't it?" I said. "I feel pretty sure that it's authentic, but we'll have the experts look at it. I'm coming back tomorrow. Are you still planning on some sort of weekend party?"

"If you'll be here, I will," she said.

"Good. By the way, you've heard of Raimundo Perrola, the Monican diplomat, haven't you?"

"That—" she began. Then she must have remembered what I'd said, for she changed her tone of voice. "Oh, yes."

"Well, he has been most helpful. It just happens that he's going to be in New York, and I thought you might invite him out for the weekend so that you can thank him personally."

"I might?" she said. I could just imagine the face she was making. I knew her opinion of Perrola and all men like him. "Of course, that's a wonderful idea. Invite him, by all means."

"Good," I said. "I'll probably see you tomorrow night. Good-bye." I hung up and looked at Perrola. "You're invited for this weekend."

"Splendid," he said. "I'll tell you what. Instead of taking the commercial airline, why don't you come with me? I fly my own plane, you know, and we can make it even faster than the airline will. Then I always keep a car at Idlewild and I can drive you out to her place. How about it?"

"I'd like that," I said, which was certainly the understatement of the year.

"You know," he said, "there's really no reason why I can't leave tonight. That way, we could be there in the morning and have a longer weekend."

"I'm afraid I can't," I said. "There are a few things I wanted to do today, and I have a ten o'clock appointment tomorrow with the Generalissimo. I want to show him the manuscript, which will be named after him, and I promised him that I would look at his private museum."

"Ah, yes," Perrola said. "His Excellency is like a small boy with that museum. Let me see, you'll be through about ten-thirty. We can drive right out to my plane and take off. I'll send the mechanic out earlier to fill the tanks and warm it up. We can be at Idlewild by seven in the evening, perhaps earlier."

"That suits me fine," I said. "Then I'll see you in the morning."

"Call me later," he said. "If you're free, perhaps we can arrange some sort of party for your last night here. Now, I'd better get to work so everything will be in order when I leave."

I took the hint and said good-bye and got out of there. I was feeling pretty good. Now there was really only one thing left to do. It was the trickiest of all, but I felt that if I kept it simple, it might work.

I told Luis I wanted to go for a long drive in the country. He headed out of the city and onto the highway. He kept asking if I didn't want to go up into the hills, but I told him to stay on the highway.

"We can't stay on this highway much longer, Don Milo," he said about an hour later. "It ends here."

I looked and saw he was right. The highway just ended. Beyond it there were a number of concrete posts, and beyond them there were a number of barrack-like buildings.

"What's that over there?" I asked. I was pretty sure I knew the answer; at least, I'd planned it for what I thought was the answer.

"Haiti," he said.

"Good," I said. "That's where I want to go."

"But that is impossible," he said. "It is not permitted. And I would be arrested the minute I set foot across the border."

"Then stop at the end of the highway and I'll walk over," I said. "I think I can go in all right. At least, I hope so."

"But why?"

I grinned at him. "I want to make a couple of phone calls and I don't want some character listening in."

He stopped at the end of the highway and I got out and walked up to the concrete posts that marked the boundary. I stopped there. I didn't want to cross over until I was sure it was all right. I yelled toward the barracks, and after a while a young officer came out. He looked at me and then walked leisurely over to the boundary. He asked me in French what I wanted.

I told him who I was. I showed him my passport and my reserve commission in the U.S. Army. And I told him that I wanted to cross into his country and make several phone calls to America, for which I would, of course, pay.

"But why?" he asked.

I grinned at him. "I've discovered that people in the Monican Republic have the habit of listening in on phone conversations. I like to talk privately."

He grinned back. "I will have to speak to my commanding officer about it," he said. "One moment."

He went back to the barracks and disappeared inside. He was gone several minutes and then he came back.

"He says that it is highly irregular, but since you are an American army officer, he will consent to it."

I stepped across the border and accompanied him back to

the barracks. There he introduced me to his commanding officer, a colonel who had been trained by the United States Army. This made us practically fraternity brothers, so he didn't mind helping me out. He took me into his office and indicated that it was mine. Then he went out, closing the door so that I could be alone with the telephone.

First I put through a call to a certain building in Washington, D.C. General Sam Roberts was one of the three men who headed up the Central Intelligence Agency. I had been recalled by the Army several times and assigned to the CIA. Before that, during the war, I had been in the OSS with General Roberts.

"March," he said when he came on the phone, "what the devil are you doing in Haiti?"

"Calling you, sir," I said. I threw in the "sir" because he liked that stuff and I wanted a favor. "I just came over here to put through this call. For the past week I've been in the Monican Republic."

"Oh," he said. "Working?"

"Yeah," I said. "On a missing man case. The one from New York. Are you interested in it?"

"Somewhat," he said carefully. "The dead pilot used to be an Army officer. I understand that another agency is even more interested in it." I knew he meant the FBI.

"Generalissimo's youngest son is in a military school somewhere in the United States," I said. "Would you know where?"

"Westlake," he said.

"I'd like to ask a favor of you, sir," I said. "And when I get back, I'll be glad to give you all the information I have."

"What's the favor?" he asked. The mention of a favor made him sound more brass than usual.

"Get the commandant of Westlake to phone the Generalissimo tomorrow morning at exactly twenty minutes past ten and talk to him about his son's progress. That's all."

"Why do you want that? No, better not tell me," he added hastily. "Knowing you, I'm sure if you told me I'd have to refuse. It's highly irregular, but I guess perhaps I can do it. Unofficially. I went to West Point with the commandant. But you'll come to Washington and give me a full report when you return?"

"Yes, sir."

"All right, March. I'll do it. But unofficially, remember."

"Yes, sir," I repeated. I thanked him and hung up. Next I put in a call to Martin Raymond at Intercontinental.

"Hi, boy," he said, coming on the phone. "What's the Haiti bit?"

"Safe place to make a phone call," I said.

"Oh. How's it going?"

"Good, I think," I said. "I expect to be back sometime tomorrow night. With a good book to read, I hope. But you'd better send me an extra five hundred dollars today. To the hotel. Send it personally, not from the company."

"Good heavens, Milo," he said. "That'll make two thousand dollars in expenses."

"Plus a hundred a day," I told him. "But if it works, you'll save seventy-two thousand dollars. That's a lot of cabbage."

"All right," he said wearily. "But you better deliver, boy."

"Sure," I said. "I'll see you around." I hung up, waited a couple of minutes, and put in a call to Lieutenant Johnny Rockland.

"Hi, Johnny," I said when he came on. "What's new?"

"You called to ask me?" he said. "How are you doing?"

"I don't know," I said. "I haven't got the score card yet. But if all goes well I'll be back in New York tomorrow night. Stick around in your office until I phone you. I should get into Idlewild about seven."

"My wife will love you," he said. "You coming on a scheduled flight?"

"No. Perrola's bringing me."

He whistled. "What's the pitch?"

"I'll tell you when I phone," I said. "Just stand by." I told him about Juana Ramos, asked him to call Miami, and hung up. I went out and found the officer. He checked with the operator on the cost of the three calls and I paid him. Then he brought out a bottle of brandy and offered me a drink. We drank toasts to the U.S. Army and the Haitian Army. I was going to be polite and offer one to the Haitian president, but then I remembered they were apt to change hourly, so I skipped it.

I left after the second drink and went back across the border to Luis and the car. He'd almost given me up for lost. We turned around and drove back to the city. I stopped at the hotel and filled up the hypodermic again and went up to the shack to give Carnicero his shot. Then back to the hotel. I told Luis to go home and get to sleep, but to be back at the hotel an hour before daylight the following morning. He nodded glumly and left. I went upstairs and went to bed myself.

I slept about four hours that afternoon. Then I got up and showered and shaved. I checked downstairs. The five hundred dollars had arrived by cable. I went down and cashed it and got Hernando to bring me up a fresh bottle of Canadian Club and some ice. After a couple of drinks I ordered some food.

A little later, I phoned Perrola. He said he had a party all set up for us and he'd pick me up about eight. I agreed.

It was some party. That much I had to give him. And he didn't want to call it quits, but I finally managed to get away by four in the morning. By that time, we were Raimundo and Milo to each other. I was really moving in fast company.

When I got back to the hotel, there was no point in going to bed. I took a shower and had another drink. Then I packed all of my things, except the manuscript. I looked at the cover again and decided the color was close enough to pass. When it was about time for Luis to show up, I mixed another dose of Pentothal and filled the hypodermic.

Luis was prompt, although he didn't look happy about it. We went down to the car and I told him to drive to the shack.

"There's just one thing, Luis," I said as he started. "If you don't like what's going to happen, you can turn the car over to me. But I'm going to move the cargo from the shack. If you want to drive me, I'll do all the work and you can just look straight ahead so you won't see what it is."

"I'll drive you," he said. "Where do we go with … it?"

"You know where Perrola keeps his plane?"

He nodded.

"That's the place. Do you know if he keeps guards around it?"

"No guards," he said. "Who would bother something that belongs to Perrola? Besides, I think he keeps it locked up."

"Good."

He glanced at me. "You know, a strange thing, Don Milo. Last night I went to report to Carnicero as usual, but he was not in his office. He had not been all day."

"I guess even a cop needs a day off once in a while," I said.

"No one knows where he is," he said. "And they found his car at the airport."

"Maybe he skipped with the family funds," I suggested.

"You were at the airport night before last," he said.

"Yeah," I said. "Seeing a friend off."

"You remember asking me about the Ramos girl?" he said. "If she worked for Carnicero? I heard that she is missing, too."

"They probably eloped," I said cheerfully. "Very romantic, you Latinos."

He made a disgusted noise in his throat and shut up. We arrived at the shack a few minutes later. I got out and unlocked the door. "Remember, Luis," I said. "Eyes to the front."

"Do not worry, Don Milo," he said. "I do not wish to see the results of your labor."

I went inside and used the hypodermic on Carnicero. Then I waited until it worked and his body grew limp again. I glanced out of the door. Luis was sitting stiffly, looking straight ahead. There was no one else in sight. The back door of the car was open. I carried Carnicero out and put him on the floor in the back. I closed the door and got up front with Luis.

"And away we go," I said.

He started the motor and drove off. "And what happens if the police should happen to stop us?" he asked.

"Obey all the laws," I said, "and they won't. But if they should, I suggest that you start driving as fast as you can and don't stop until we hit another country."

"Very romantic, you *norteamericanos*," he said sarcastically.

I laughed and leaned back on the seat, feeling the tension building up in me as the time drew nearer.

From the look of the sky, it lacked about a half hour to daylight when we reached the private landing field where Luis said Perrola kept his plane. There was a large hangar at one end of the field. Luis drove up and stopped in front of it. I got out and went over to the doors. They were locked with a huge padlock. It took only a minute to pick it. I went inside, closing the doors after me. I'd brought a flashlight along and I didn't want the light showing outside. I switched it on and examined the plane.

It was a converted B-29. Looking inside, I could see that it had been made pretty luxurious. I walked around, checking it. Back in the tail, they had walled off a luggage section. The entrance to it was in the belly. That was locked, too. I picked it and looked inside. It was good and roomy. It would have held several trunks.

I went back out to the car and carried Carnicero inside. I boosted him up through the door into the luggage compartment. I looked around the hangar until I found some wire. I climbed up into the compartment and lashed Carnicero to one side so he wouldn't roll around. I dropped to the ground and closed and locked the door in the belly of the ship.

I thought it ought to work. Perrola wouldn't be carrying enough luggage on this trip to bother with the luggage compartment. It would be easier to put it in the main part of the plane. I went back outside and locked the outer doors. I climbed in the car and told Luis to take us back to the hotel. It was just beginning to get light.

When we reached the hotel, I had Luis come up with me. I ordered both of us some breakfast from room service and poured myself another drink. I offered Luis one, but he didn't want it.

"Don Milo," he said, "you are going to leave soon, yes?"

"Today, if I'm lucky," I said. "You will be happy?"

"Yes and no," he said. "It is true that you have made a nervous wreck out of me. It will be months before I again feel safe. But I must confess I have enjoyed it, too. There are no hard feelings about that day on the mountain?"

"No hard feelings, Luis."

"Good. And someday perhaps I will know what has happened the last two days."

"I imagine you will," I said.

"I wonder," he said slyly, "if I am still working for Carnicero ..."

"Not if he's run away," I said. "But if he's done that, you and your cousin should be able to find some way of lifting his bank account and making it look as if he took it with him."

For a minute an interested look appeared on his face, then was replaced by one of horror. *"Qué diablos,"* he said. "How can you put such ideas in my head? It is in this way you have corrupted me. Even if Carnicero were dead, it would not be safe to steal his money. Torcido will want to steal it himself."

I laughed and went to open the door for the waiter, who had just knocked. We had our breakfast and then just rested until it was time to go to the Palace. I let Luis take my suitcase, and I tucked the manuscript under my arm. I hadn't slept all night, but I felt all keyed up as we went downstairs. I checked out at the desk and paid my bill. We went out to the car and Luis drove straight to the Palace. I told him to wait and went in.

It was exactly ten when the secretary again ushered me in to see the dictator of the Monican Republic. The old man stood up to greet me and shook hands with me as I reached his desk.

There was a subtle difference in his attitude, and I knew why. He was beginning to think that they had been wrong. I had said that I was there to find a manuscript; I had apparently found it and was now leaving. There had been nothing in any of the reports to indicate that I was interested in Moreno, except perhaps that I had once been with the sister of the rebel in prison. But she was a pretty girl and that was understandable. Even a trusted agent like Carnicero, the old man was thinking, could make a mistake.

I showed him the manuscript, commenting on the fact that someone had put a cover on it. He leafed through it, feeling the paper and peering at the script.

"It is certainly very old," he said. "Perhaps it is what it seems to be. I am almost sorry that I gave you permission to take it away, but I did not think you would really find it."

"It will honor you wherever it is," I said.

"*Claro que sí,*" he said.

"I am flying back today with Señor Perrola," I said.

"Yes, I know," he said. "Come. I will show you the rest of my museum."

I followed him to the other room, glancing at my watch. It was a quarter past ten. I held the manuscript firmly beneath my arm.

He started at the front and began to work back, showing me the things in the cases. Most of them were personal, meaningless things. There were all the various uniforms he had worn as he promoted himself up through his own army. There were medals from many countries. There was a tiny Monican colonel's uniform that had been made for one of his sons when a child. There were trophies. There were framed letters from the heads of other countries.

I was beginning to get nervous.

Then the door opened and there was the secretary. "I am sorry, Generalissimo," he said, "but there is a phone call from General Hodges. I knew you'd want to take it."

The old man had started to frown at the interruption, but the name cleared the frown away. "You will excuse me, Señor March," he said, "but I wish to take this call. Leonardo here will show you the other things." He strode quickly out of the room.

This wasn't quite the way I'd wanted it to happen, but the secretary obviously wasn't going to leave. He walked back to join me. I saw him glance at the table where the Moreno manuscript was and a worried look came over his face.

"This table," he said, walking over to it, "contains things which have been threats against the Generalissimo." As he reached it, he casually turned the Moreno manuscript over so that the title wouldn't show, trying to mask the action with his body. "It includes some weapons which were used in actual attempts on his life."

"Yes," I said casually. I moved down until I was standing beside him. "The Generalissimo told me about them the other day." I leaned forward to peer at one of the glass doors. There was a large gold cup back of it. "What is that?" I asked. "It looks interesting."

The secretary seemed relieved at having the conversation move away from the table. He went to the glass case with alacrity and opened the door.

It took three seconds. As he reached for the door, I took the manuscript from beneath my arm and exchanged it for the one on the table. I tucked the new manuscript under my arm with the title next to my body. Then I was over beside the clerk as he took the cup from the case.

"The Generalissimo won this cup at the International Horse Show ten years ago," he said. "He is an excellent rider and has won many cups." He held it up for my examination.

During the next few minutes the secretary droned on and on about the things in the museum, but I barely heard him. I merely made the proper sounds of awe whenever he stopped. Right then, I wanted to get out of there more than I'd ever wanted anything in my life. I felt like starting to run. Instead, I followed him around and made noises.

"I believe that is everything," the secretary finally said.

Just then the dictator came back. My mouth was dry as he entered the room. I wondered if he would be suspicious. But his gaze merely swept idly around the room and came back to me.

"That was the commandant of the military school my youngest son attends," he said. "He called to tell me what excellent progress Rafael is making. I am pleased. Did Leonardo show you the rest of the museum?"

"Everything," I said. "This is certainly a great monument to your life and work."

"Yes," he said. "It will go into a state museum after I am dead." He stared fiercely off into space as though to deny that death could interrupt his power.

"It should be a great inspiration to your people," I said solemnly. "Now, I'm afraid I've kept you too long, and I must be going to meet Señor Perrola."

"And I must get back to my duties," he said. He led the way back into the office, and the secretary and I followed. "Señor March, I am happy that your mission has been so successful. It is an interesting document you have found." He stared at the manuscript under my arm and my heart stopped beating, or so it seemed, for I thought he was going to ask to see it again.

"We will send you a copy of the expert's report," I said hurriedly. "And I thank you for your many kindnesses that have made this possible. I trust you will forgive my taking so much of your time."

"It is I who must apologize for not giving you more time," he said. "I would like nothing better than to sit down and pore over that manuscript with you. I know the old Spanish very well. But then we are both busy men. *Adiós,* Señor March."

"*Adiós,* Your Excellency," I said. I turned and followed the secretary out of the office. I finally managed a deep breath when I reached the corridor, but only one. I wasn't even out of the Palace yet. I thanked the secretary and went down the hall to Perrola's office. He was waiting for me.

"Ah, there you are," he said. He looked as fresh and rested as if there had been no party the night before. "Too bad you didn't stay last night. We had much fun after you left."

"I have enough of a head as it is," I said. "You don't look as if it bothered you."

"Parties never bother me," he said. "One cannot be a diplomat and have hangovers. Is that your famous manuscript?"

"Yes," I said. I hurried on before he could get the idea of wanting to look at it. "Shall we go? I have my driver and car waiting in front."

"We'll go in my car," he said. "Why don't you go on down and settle with him, and I'll bring my car around?"

"Fine," I said. I resisted the impulse to run again and walked slowly out of the office with him. In the corridor he went one way, I went the other. I went out past numerous guards, holding my breath as I passed each one. Finally I reached Luis and the car, feeling weak.

The first thing I did was to get in the back, unfasten my suitcase, and put the manuscript inside. I closed it again. The manuscript was too much of a temptation for everyone when it was in view. I put my suitcase on the ground.

"Perrola is going to drive me," I told Luis, "so this is our good-bye." I pulled out some money and separated three hundred and twenty-five dollars.

"Here is your pay for today, Luis, and a bonus of three hundred dollars. I suggest that you consider yourself working for me at least another day. It is true, of course, that you might find someone willing to pay more than three hundred for the things you could say, but I don't advise it. Sooner or later, they would get to thinking and realize that you must have had more to do with it than you admit. You understand that?"

"Don Milo, you are my friend and patron," he said reproachfully. "Would I do such a thing to you?"

"If the price was right."

"For no price," he cried. "Could I spend it in the grave?"

"True," I said. "Well, good-bye, Luis." I held out my hand.

"Go with God," he said. "Life will be much easier, but I will miss you."

"And my money," I said with a grin.

He climbed back into the car, gave me a merry grin, and drove away. Perrola came around the corner in a little sports car a few seconds later. I got in with my suitcase and we were off in a roar. The way Perrola drove, I almost expected the sports car to leave the ground and fly to New York.

The plane was already out on the field, the motors idling, when we arrived. There was a man beside it. He came over and took our luggage and put it in the plane. Up front. Perrola and I climbed into the plane, and Perrola nodded through the windshield to the man. A moment later, he pushed the throttle forward and the big plane started rolling across the field, picking up speed. Then we were in the air almost before I knew it.

I leaned back in my seat and breathed a sigh of relief. I felt as limp as a rag now that it was over. Or almost over. Now all I had to worry about was a radio message.

ELEVEN

It was a pleasant enough trip, if you can call eight hours of waiting for something to happen pleasant. But no radio messages came through. There was one period when Perrola worried about the fact that the tail of his plane seemed heavy, but after a time he forgot about that. The rest of the way we talked about women—or, rather, Perrola talked about women and I grunted.

It was just seven o'clock when we arrived at Idlewild. We got out with our luggage and somebody took over the plane, trundling it to a hangar. We went in and went through customs. The U.S. Customs men were more thorough than those in the Monican Republic. They found the guns, but I had a permit, so that was all right. We got into a small argument about the manuscript because it was written in Spanish, but I finally managed to convince them because inside on the flyleaf Dr. Moreno had put his address as New York University. Fortunately, Perrola was with another inspector several feet away and didn't hear any of this.

"I think," I said when we finally got away, "I'd better call Miss Mellany and tell her we're here and on our way."

"Excellent," he said. "I'll get my car and bring it around to the front entrance. You can meet me there with our luggage."

"Okay," I said.

He took off and I went to the phone booth. I dialed the number. It was already too late for that switchboard, so it was Johnny Rockland who answered the phone.

"Nice of you to wait up," I said. "I hope you kept dinner hot."

He gave me a short summation of my character. "You in town?" he asked.

"Idlewild," I told him. "While I'm at it, you might ask some of your brother cops to take a look in the luggage compartment of Perrola's plane. There's a door in the belly. They'll find an illegal alien in there. He's a little indisposed, but you can certainly book him for illegal entry while you talk to him about other things. And I would question him fast; he's had a lot of Pentothal in the last two days, which might make him talk a little more."

"It all sounds highly illegal," he said. "Who would do a thing like that?"

"How do I know?" I asked innocently. "I'm just an honest citizen giving you a little tip."

"Would you have any idea who he is, Honest Citizen?" he asked.

"His name is Jorge Carnicero and he's the Chief of Police of Puerto Torcido," I said. "Sometimes he's known as El Nariz. Oh, yes, and in the pocket of his coat you'll find a gun. You might want to look it over."

"You're not kidding?" he asked.

"I'm not kidding."

"Milo, I love you," he said. "And I don't want to know any more about it. Anything else?"

"Yeah, there was something," I said. "Oh, yes, do you know what kind of car Perrola keeps in New York?"

"Yeah. A red Mercedes-Benz. Why?"

"Nothing important," I said. "He and I are about to start for Westport, Connecticut. I understand he's a very fast driver. You know me; I'm the timid sort. Why don't you arrange to have the traffic officers keep an eye out for him?"

"What good will it do? He has diplomatic immunity."

"I've heard. Why don't you try it anyway? And have a little confidence in your Uncle Milo."

"Okay. Will do. You've earned that much."

"And Johnny ..."

"Yeah?"

"Why don't you manage to be at the nearest precinct? And then think fast. Good-bye, pal. Give my regards to the taxpayers." I hung up.

Then I got the luggage and went out front. Perrola was already there, in a red Mercedes-Benz. I threw the luggage in the back and then climbed in beside him.

"What did she say?" he asked.

"Tickled to death that we're here," I said. "Know how to get to Westport?"

"Of course," he said. The Mercedes-Benz took off with a roar.

I have to say one thing for that boy. Nobody could ever accuse him of paying any attention to speed laws. Half the time the speedometer was hovering around one hundred and I was keeping my fingers crossed. It was going to play hell with everything if we got stopped by the wrong cop. But for once the angels were with me. As Luis would have said, I must have been living right.

We left Long Island and crossed Upper Manhattan. We were just about at the thruway and making a good seventy-five on a city street when a siren screamed behind us and the red light started blinking. Perrola cursed beneath his breath and pulled to the side of the street. The patrol car cut in front of us and stopped. One of the officers got out and came back.

"In a hurry, wasn't you?" he asked.

"Yes," Perrola said. He sounded as if he were talking to the office boy.

"Let me see your license," the cop said. He was used to it.

"Of course," Perrola said. He got out his license and handed it over.

"While you're looking at it, officer, you might notice that I'm an ambassador of the Monican Republic. In simple language, I have diplomatic immunity."

"Yeah," the cop said, taking the license.

This was my cue. "Raimundo," I said, tugging at his sleeve.

"Yes?" he asked.

"Do you mind if I tell you something?"

"What?"

"We were only doing seventy-five, and the fine on it can't be more than maybe fifty dollars. It's not much money. Waive your immunity and pay it."

"Why?" he asked arrogantly.

"Merry Mellany," I said, "comes from old American stock. She's very proud of the fact that her family came here in 1640. That kind of thing does funny things to some Americans.

Her, for example. She's got all kinds of pull, but she insists on paying every little parking ticket she gets. And I've heard her rave against people who use pull to get out of paying fines. This would be a good chance to make a hit with her. If you waive your immunity and pay the fine, it'll go over big with her." He was silent for a minute. I could almost hear the wheels clicking in his head. I held my breath.

"Maybe it is a good idea," he said. "What is fifty dollars? You are sure about this, Milo?"

"Positive," I said. "I've heard her enough times."

"I will do it," he said, and I took another deep breath.

"Yeah, I guess you're right," the cop said, handing the license back through the window.

"Of course I'm right," Perrola said. "However, officer, I have decided to waive my immunity. After all, the laws of your country should be obeyed."

"Yeah?" the cop said unbelievingly. He recovered quickly. "Okay, tell your pal to go up and get in the squad car. I'll ride with you. We'll go to the precinct."

"But why?" Perrola asked. "Don't you just give me a ticket?"

"Not on this one, buddy. You were doing seventy-five in a twenty-five-mile zone. Let's go."

I got out and went up to the squad car. I didn't say anything to the cop and we rode back to the precinct in silence. When we got there, the four of us went inside. Lieutenant Rockland was standing talking to the desk sergeant. He didn't even look at me.

The traffic cop explained the whole thing to the desk sergeant and he asked Perrola if it was true that he waived his diplomatic immunity. Perrola said impatiently that it was. At that point, Johnny Rockland stepped forward and arrested him for murder. It was real pretty, and I was proud of Johnny for being so quick on the uptake.

For a minute, I thought Perrola was going to slug somebody and take off. Then he looked at me and you could see he'd figured it out. If there ever was a double whammy, it was in his eyes when he stared at me. He was demanding a lawyer as they led him away.

Then I went into session with Johnny. I gave him the photostat of Perrola's bank account and the $130,000 deposit. I told him everything that I knew and suspected.

"All you've got is a fighting chance," I told him. "Maybe between the two of them you can prove something. Maybe not. But you've got them."

"A chance is all I want," he said grimly. He went to the phone and made a call. "The boys have El Nariz on ice," he said when he came back. "He's doing some talking, but not enough yet. But we may be able to use what he's said as a lever. They've sent the gun over to be checked. That ought to give us something. The boys say he has a pretty badly busted nose."

"Probably fell down," I said.

"You're a little marked yourself," he said.

"Shaving," I said. "You know they don't have those good American blades in foreign countries."

"Yeah," he said dryly. "Will you come in tomorrow and repeat everything you've told me, for the record?"

"Sure," I said.

"Okay," he said. "Now I'll go to work. Thanks, Milo."

"I did it for the taxpayers," I said gravely.

He went off and I used the phone to call Martin Raymond at home. I told him I had the manuscript and to relax. I'd deliver it to him on Monday morning. Then I called Ben Brackett at home and told him what happened to his $130,000 and that the cops had the photostat. The rest was up to him.

It was a little more than two hours since we had entered the precinct. I was tired. I picked up my suitcase, grinned at the desk sergeant, and went out. I looked around for a cab.

An orange taxi swooped in to the curb. "Taxi, mister?" the driver asked.

"You're as welcome as the flowers in May," I told him. I opened the door and climbed in. "Take me to—"

"Pay no attention to him, driver," another voice cut in. 'Take us to Westport, Connecticut. And don't spare the cylinders."

"Yes, ma'am," the driver said.

I knew who it was without looking around. "Hello, Merry," I said. "How did you get here?"

"I was way ahead of you, buster," she said. "I knew you wouldn't bring that horrible Perrola person to my place, so you must have some plan. So I used some of my connections, which finally got me to a Lieutenant Rockland. So I knew where you were."

"My friend," I muttered under my breath.

"Here," she said. "I brought a thermos full of dry martinis." She handed me a large thermos jug.

I took it with pleasure. "My," I said, "I didn't know that you were the home type. Where are my slippers?"

"Here, dear," she said. And I'll be damned if she didn't hand me a pair of slippers.

"Anything else?" I asked.

"Yes," she said. "Have yourself a couple of martinis, then put your head in my lap. It's Friday night. Everything else will keep until Monday."

You know, I thought she was right. I had a couple of generous slugs of martini and then I put my head in her lap and went to sleep while the taxi roared on toward Westport, its meter clicking merrily.

AFTERWORD

"This Is a Work of Fiction"

This novel, set in an imaginary Caribbean island nation called the Monican Republic, or the Republic of Santa Monica (yuk yuk), has features and characters in common with a real case in the Dominican Republic under the dictatorship of Rafael Trujillo.

Jesús Galíndez

The fictional NYU professor Dr. Jaime Moreno, whose scandalous manuscript Milo recovers, resembles Jesús de Galíndez, who wrote his own exposé of the Trujillo dictatorship while teaching at Columbia University. Galíndez vanished from the streets of New York City in 1956 before his book was to be published. His fate has never been thoroughly solved, but he is believed to have been smuggled into the Dominican Republic and then tortured and murdered by Trujillo's henchman.

The man who is believed to have kidnapped Galíndez was Gerald Lester Murphy, an American pilot for the Dominican airline. It was claimed that Murphy later died accidentally by falling off a cliff as a result of a fight with another pilot,

Octavio de la Maza. The latter was arrested and imprisoned despite his protestations of innocence. He later was found hanged in his cell, seeming to have left a note expressing remorse for Murphy's death, which was taken as his confession of both murder and suicide.

Raimundo Perrola was undoubtedly modeled on Porfirio Rubirosa, an international playboy and a diplomat (and possible assassin) in Trujillo's regime. (Interestingly, a forensic historian, Daniel J. Voelker, speculated in an article titled "Will the Real James Bond Please Stand Up?" that Rubirosa was the main inspiration for Ian Fleming's James Bond. Ironically, a real-life character in the Milo March novel *Wild Midnight Falls*—Richard Sorge—has been called the Communist James Bond.)

With such similarities to true events and people, one might expect the author to have added a disingenuous disclaimer to the front matter, as many writers do ("Any resemblance to actual events or persons, living or dead, is entirely coincidental"). Maybe Ken Crossen felt that the comparisons were so obvious that it would be silly to claim that this is merely a work of fiction. But of course, the novel is not a true story, and much of it is made up. (For example, I have not found a likely model for the character with a large nose.)

Although FBI investigations appeared to expose the Dominican version of events as false, the Murphy and de la Maza deaths were never definitively solved. Rafael Trujillo was assassinated in 1961, about three years after the publication of *The Gallows Garden*.

Kendra Crossen Burroughs

ABOUT THE AUTHOR

Kendell Foster Crossen (1910–1981), the only child of Samuel Richard Crossen and Clo Foster Crossen, was born on a farm outside Albany in Athens County, Ohio—a village of some 550 souls in the year of this birth. His ancestors on his mother's side include the 19th-century songwriter Stephen Collins Foster ("Oh! Susanna"); William  Allen, founder of Allentown, Pennsylvania; and Ebenezer Foster, one of the Minute Men who sprang to arms at the Lexington alarm in April 1775.

Ken went to Rio Grande College on a football scholarship but stayed only one year. "When I was fairly young, I developed the disgusting habit of reading," says Milo March, and it seems Ken Crossen, too, preferred self-education. He loved literature and poetry; favorite authors included Christopher Marlowe and Robert Service. He also enjoyed participant sports and was a semi-pro fighter in the heavyweight class. He became a practicing magician and had a passion for chess.

After college Ken wrote several one-act plays that were produced in a small Cleveland theater. He worked in steel mills and Fisher Body plants. Then he was employed as an insurance investigator, or "claims adjuster," in Cleveland. But he left the job and returned to the theater, now as a performer: a tumbling clown in the Tom Mix Circus; a comic and carnival barker for a tent show, and an actor in a medicine show.

In 1935, Ken hitchhiked to New York City with a typewriter under his arm, and found work with the WPA Writers' Project, covering cricket for the *New York City Guidebook*. In 1936, he was hired by the Munsey Publishing Company as associate editor of the popular *Detective Fiction Weekly*. The company asked him to come up with a character to compete with The Shadow, and thus was born a unique superhero of pulps, comic books, and radio—The Green Lama, an American mystic trained in Tibetan Buddhism.

Crossen sold his first story, "The Aaron Burr Murder Case," to *Detective Fiction Weekly* in September 1939, but says he didn't begin to make a living from writing till 1941. He tried his hand at publishing true crime magazines, comics, and a picture magazine, without great success, so he set out for Hollywood. From his typewriter flowed hundreds of stories, short novels for magazines, scripts radio, television, and film, nonfiction articles. He delved into science fiction in the 1950s, starting with "Restricted Clientele" (February 1951). His dystopian novels *Year of Consent* and *The Rest Must Die* also appeared in this decade.

In the course of his career Ken Crossen acquired six pseud-onyms: Richard Foster, Bennett Barlay, Kent Richards, Clay Richards, Christopher Monig, and M.E. Chaber. The variety was necessary because different publishers wanted to reserve specific bylines for their own publications. Ken based "M.E. Chaber" on the Hebrew word for "author," *mechaber.*

In the early '50s, as M.E. Chaber, Crossen began to write a series of full-length mystery/espionage novels featuring Milo March, an insurance investigator. The first, *Hangman's Harvest,* was published in 1952. In all, there are twenty-two Milo March novels. One, *The Man Inside,* was made into a British film starring Jack Palance.

Most of Ken's characters were private detectives, and Milo was the most popular. Paperback Library reissued twenty-five Crossen titles in 1970–1971, with covers by Robert McGin-nis. Twenty were Milo March novels, four featured an insur-ance investigator named Brian Brett, and one was about CIA agent Kim Locke.

Crossen excelled at producing well-plotted entertainment with fast-moving action. His research skills were a strong asset, back when research meant long hours searching library microfilms and poring over street maps and hotel floorplans. His imagination took him to many international hot spots, although he himself never traveled abroad. Like Milo March, he hated flying ("When you've seen one cloud, you've seen them all").

Ken Crossen was married four times. With his first wife he had three children (Stephen, Karen, Kendra) and with his second a son (David). He lived in New York, Florida, Southern California, Nevada, and other parts of the country. Milo March moves from Denver to New York City after five books of the series, with an apartment on Perry Street in Greenwich Village; that's where Ken lived, too. His and Milo's favorite watering hole was the Blue Mill Tavern, a short walk from the apartment.

Ken Crossen was a combination of many of the traits of his different male characters: tough, adventuresome, with a taste for gin and shapely women. But perhaps the best observation was made in an obituary written by sci-fi writer Avram Davidson, who described Ken as a fundamentally gentle person who had been buffeted by many winds.